Kinky Playwright

by

T.G. Hyde

To

Best wishes!

Mari...

from

Glenn

2022.

Awduresau Cymru Publishing
18 Seaview Terrace
Swansea SA1 6FE

T G Hyde

Originally from Merthyr Tydfil, Glenn Hyde has been based in Swansea for around fifteen years. He was educated at both Swansea University and The University of Glamorgan, gaining a first class honours Batchelor of Arts degree in History.

Glenn has previously released a collection of short stories called Dark or Bitter, and he is currently working on another selection of short works.

PROLOGUE

The Kinky Playwright they called me. How, you may ask politely, does a respectable, almost-middle-aged man come to acquire that particular moniker/epithet/tag? (Delete where appropriate). I say *almost* middle aged, because I'm about to turn forty, and I don't feel young anymore, but I certainly don't feel old either. I just feel...redundant. No, worn out...no, no...wiped out. It was Gogol...no, not Gogol. Tolstoy? No, let me just get this right...it was...Dostoyevsky. Yes, Dostoyevsky wrote of the '...*fools and the scoundrels who live beyond forty!*'....No, stop, man! Don't start this with some flighty quote! Dear me, I sound so pretentious, don't I? I'm only a couple of sentences in, and here I am paraphrasing one of the greats of Russian literature within a few lines of my strange tale. I haven't really read any Dostoyevsky, I just read that line the other day when I was flicking through an old copy of *Notes from Underground* at a bookstore.

5

Come to think of it though, that was written a hundred and fifty years ago. I can't imagine many living that long then, especially in Russia....Jesus here we go, I'm waffling again, digressing as they say, forever the quasi-intellectual, especially in print...oh come on, stick to it man. Stick to the plot, for once in your life! Well, forty though! What's forty these days? So, I'm almost there, and I'm very certainly a fool. In my case, I've become *branded* with the title of a fool indeed. Oh I've certainly been branded, branded for life. Haunted by it in fact. People, kids, pointing at me in the street, mocking me, laughing at me. That's what they did...

Anyway, put the handkerchief away you...fool...knob...foolish, stupid fucking knob that I am! Definitely a fool, but not a scoundrel. No, I don't deserve sympathy, but I'm not really asking for it...am I? Then why this? No I'm not. I am a good man though...honestly I am. Right, where was I?

Back to it. Yes, how, might you ask, am I now forever known as The Kinky Playwright?

The Kinky fucking Playwright for fuck's sake! Sorry, I might as well add the fucking and the rest of it. Vent my fucking anger! It's not going to make it any worse for me now, that's for sure. My work, my writing, none of it was in any way kinky, or even sexually driven. Pervy Novelist might not have had any wings - they're all fucking perverts. But kinky playwright, that had connotations. *The Singing Detective, Pennies from heaven*, you know… louche, leftie types.

I was no Dennis Potter. Oh no, I'm not beginning to compare myself to Dennis Potter in greatness, depth of imagination, or what I now refer to as 'natural imagination.' I mean, well, I could compare myself, but then, my inspiration came from …something else. Or somewhere else. No, I was just using his work as an example of what I would regard as primal, or kinky, as well as being ground-breaking and funny.   But it wasn't the content of my work that ended up getting me branded - yes, branded - with that bloody awful and sickening title by the bloody media and the rest of those bastards. No, it was the events, or the… inspiration, for want of a better, or more faithful, description behind the concept of my ideas and my writing.

I know I would want to know how and why all this came about. I suppose that betrays my inquisitive and dissatisfied nature. Although they are traits that should have helped me with my profession, rather than get me into this life-shattering mess. 'The nosy wee bastard', as my Scottish grandfather would often refer to me.

'You'd make a good detective my boy, or an investigative journalist. Don't just become a dreamer,' he would say.

I used to imagine Sherlock Holmes when he said detective. Firstly, because my grandfather was a great fan of Arthur Conan Doyle, and secondly, because I didn't know what an investigative journalist was when I was a kid. I wasn't the brightest. More inquisitive, more imaginative than intelligent. I probably had OCD from childhood as well. Who knows? Nothing was talked about back then, especially in our household. Still isn't, come to think of it. I would spend hours obsessing over product numbers in the toy section of my mother's catalogues. I literally made logbooks of them. It used to make my grandfather laugh. My parents just thought that I was weird. Yes, I was a strange kid, but I had a wonderful imagination.

From my teens I worked hard to get my grades, jobs, and Sarah of course. I was definitely a late developer. That wasn't surprising, considering I still spent half my time dreaming about fucking spaceships! I did eventually become a journalist though. Well, a part-time journalist… very part time actually. But not an investigative journalist. No, that would probably be pushing it a bit, if I'm going to be totally honest with you. Well, as honest as I can be. And I was also a successful writer of sorts. I also eventually became a playwright. A playwright by default you could say. I suppose to the layman a writer is a writer: a hack, a wordsmith or whatever. If it fits the bill, has a good, catchy title to sell papers from the gutter, to become click bait for the masses. Shoved between a picture of the latest hot weathergirl's cleavage and the latest Royal exposé. Hmm, not sure if that came out right.

Success? Oh yes, I tasted it. Briefly. All too briefly. I had that desire, that hunger, that drive, an inborn longing that I didn't know was there. Some might say that it's akin to a drug addiction you never planned on having. I was also happily married with a young daughter. I still have the young daughter, but the marriage is now over. I adored my wife, I really did. All will be revealed in this story, or a short and recent autobiographical account of my life up until this morning if you like. A retelling of where, or how I found my ideas. *Received* my ideas may be a better description of events.

CHAPTER 1

I had been a successful playwright for a short while. It began with a radio play that was adapted from one of my short stories. It's difficult to get into playwriting, but once you're in, it pays well and it's fairly regular work, as opposed to getting a book published every couple of years.

Before that I did my journalist stint for a regional newspaper based in the north east of England (more about that later). Yes, it was my stories that actually got me noticed to begin with. The publisher really liked a black comedy about two inept burglars set in Middlesbrough, which is very near to my hometown. I had more to offer, but things didn't turn out well after that.

Anyway, back to the radio play. This particular short story, *Stolen Goods,* was picked up by the BBC within weeks of me getting 'discovered'. The Beeb and my agent felt that the humour, crossed with the dialectical dialogue, would transfer really well to radio, and probably television.

They were right. It did transfer from radio to television, and it did do well. It set me up with some great contacts, and the offer of more work. I just needed to produce more stories and scripts at that level - or above. I could write stories, but it wasn't good work. And I certainly didn't have enough good or even decent ideas to sustain a career. Well, that's when the tensions and stress come into it, and with the tension and the stress come the migraines...and this is really where I need to begin.

My problems, well, my *big* problems, not the migraines and what they brought to me, began not long after the TV Awards thing. I had never thought of myself as a person for glamour, celebrity and all that nonsense, but now I became obsessed with it. My then-wife Sarah certainly wasn't, although she was just as attractive as any starlet we met during what now seem surreal times.

Looking back, it really was a pleasant story for Sarah and me before the problems began. We met at university in London. We were attractive, aspiring, and pretentious. Well,

I was more aspiring and pretentious, even back then. I really was a right pretentious young knob. I did my best to drop the accent, adopted a twang. I was obviously conscious - ashamed? - of my background. Fuck, it really does pain me now to think of how annoying I must have been.

Sarah was far more in the attractive bracket. Very attractive. She was always comfortable in life and in her own skin, and very tolerant of people, especially me. I, on the other hand, had always felt like I had something to prove. The grass was always greener on the other side. That's it in a nutshell I suppose.

I was from a traditional and comfortable working class background. All very humble, but comfortable, and that's more than a lot of people start from. Sarah had far better reasons than I to feel unsettled, more affected. Her life had been far from perfect. Her mother died in a car accident shortly before Sarah was due to begin University. She had been a beautiful but troubled woman. It was found that she had been three times over the drink-drive limit at the time of the crash. I suppose it was fortunate that nobody else was involved or injured.

She had been a gifted ceramic artist and was renowned in the area, and quite successful. Sarah's father Tim was her second husband. He was a charming and handsome man who worked as a logistics officer in the Royal Navy, later carrying out consultancy work. Like most families of servicemen, they moved around quite a bit.

When Sarah was fourteen, the family finally settled in Cornwall. Growing up in mainly coastal areas, Sarah, her father and her brother Alex were part of the surfing scene. The unfortunate and untimely passing of her mother had brought the three of them closer as a family. Anyway, lucky for me that they spent half their lives in and around beaches and water.

I grew up in Redcar, so I was also a native of the coast. Apart from swimming for my school and the county, I would spend most of my free time as a youth on Redcar beach, playing about and windsurfing. Funny thing is, with the snobs I met at uni, they would scoff and smirk when I would speak at length about Redcar beach. They'd never even been there, or even seen a fucking photograph of the place.

My accent was another talking point. The number of times I had to explain to them that it wasn't Geordie, it was 'Smoggy'. In fact, it was the Geordies who gave us that nickname in the first place, after the amount of smog from the industry. Back when there was industry, I might add. I found out from Sarah that the bastards would mock me behind my back, ridicule my regional dialect. So, what did I do? Did I hit back at them? Thicken my accent? Show pride in my background? No. I just adopted that neutral middle-class drone like the guys in Radiohead. Just to fit in.

I did enjoy informing them that Ian McEwan's *Atonement* was filmed in Redcar. Yes, you wankers, *that* is my home town! It would usually change their attitudes. You see, there has to be success, exposure, a connection for these people. I can vouch for that now. A connection with greatness, or someone who's got it. Although they would usually make some

15

inane remark like, 'Isn't it all just the same up there?' The great north-south divide would come right to the surface. I would sit, sullen, simmering with rage. Sarah would tell me to take no notice, because they're all clueless twats. How can you not fall in love with someone like her? She was worth a hundred of them.

So let's fast forward a bit. Sarah had inherited both her parents' good looks, talents and intelligence. I was merely passable back when we first met. Certainly nothing to shout home about. I failed my A level exams after my second attempt; I bummed around for a while, before realising that I didn't really have much to offer. Teaching was still an option, so I did an access course in my local college. I was in my mid twenties when I finally got into university. Sarah was twenty one - older than most, as she'd taken some time out due to her mother's tragic death .

I was the captain of the university's swimming team, and I liked to surf whenever I got the chance. It reminded me of those long nights on the beach back home. With the swimming and the rest, I could show off my toned physique to Sarah. That made me feel more attractive - I felt I didn't have much else to offer. There I go again, betraying the insecurities that would lead to my later 'misgivings'.

But Sarah was, and still is, a striking woman. Distinctively confident, and innately calm. I was mesmerised by her from the first time I saw her sitting in the student union bar one Saturday afternoon towards the end of our second term. At best, she was intrigued by me, but thankfully we hit it off. And, as I said, I worked on it. I worked on her. Somehow I made her laugh. I often wonder, now, if it wasn't through pity.

Yes, she was humoured by my presence to begin with, especially when my regional accent would start to corrupt my attempts at the required middle class idioms of educated folk. I had to work hard, as I usually had to in life, just to keep her interested. God, it kept me on my toes! It almost cost me my studies. I was like a lapdog who never left her side. Unlike most attractive women, she was okay with this. So I clung to her, I made it known that I could provide for her. Isn't that what women want? A nice home, children, money and a comfortable life?

We both graduated, me in education studies, and Sarah in art and philosophy. I worked my arse off. Sarah merely had to turn up. That pretty much set the tone for the rest of our time together. We found careers soon enough. After teacher training college, we both began working in adult education. I taught English and basic skills, Sarah textiles and ceramics, like her mother.

Around the same time, we had some good luck. There was a big push towards the 'help to buy' scheme aimed at first time buyers, especially professionals like us. They offered us a deposit grant on a tiny one bedroom flat. We had already lived there for nearly two years, and it was pretty rough when we first moved in. It soon became obvious that the once notorious area was quickly becoming gentrified like many other parts of the capital. We sold that place for £250,000. Yes, a quarter of a million! I dread to think what that glorified bedsit is worth now. We couldn't believe our luck. Jesus, and I still wasn't happy. Don't look a gift horse in the mouth indeed. My mother later told me the other day that from then on, I'd overlooked a 'stable full of gift horses'. Back then though, it was time to get out of the metropolis.

We decided to move down to Padstow, to be near Sarah's father and the coast. We were able to buy a nice three bedroom cottage and have about thirty grand to spare for some TLC, and we also put aside something for schooling, because we both wanted children. The money also meant Sarah wouldn't have to work for a year if she didn't want to, or, if she got bored, she could work part time. I continued to teach in the adult learning sector, but there was more travelling involved, mostly throughout the whole of Cornwall.

Then came Lorna, our only child, followed by our belated wedding vows, and two cocker-poos, Mable and Matilda. Achingly middle class isn't it? They cost us a lot of money. My dad was horrified that we had spent four grand on 'a couple of mongrels'. There again, he would also take a good beating just to save thirty pence on a pint of beer. I'd had two Staffordshire bull terriers when I was growing up, Sid and Clive, after Sid James, and Clive Dunn from *Dad's Army*. I grew up on old school comedy. My father's favourites, bless him.

So, nothing too glamorous down there in Padstow, but we were certainly comfortable for a while. After a few years, I started a master's degree in comparative literature. I wasn't really *that* intelligent, well read, or academic, but I felt I'd gone as far as I could with adult learning. We were ok for money for the time being, so maybe I could lecture part time after getting an MA or go onto a PhD…maybe that was being a bit too ambitious, maybe I was just too lazy, maybe, maybe ...

I began reading for pleasure again - science fiction classics mainly, the writers that I had loved as a teenager and as a student. H.G Wells was an early favourite. I can remember watching *The First Men on the Moon* one wintry afternoon just before Christmas at my grandparents' house. It really sent my imagination racing. A Victorian space ship! It blew me away. Then my grandfather told me about the infamous Orson Welles radio narration of the script from *War of the Worlds* back in 1938. My grandfather also told me that when it was first aired, listeners actually thought that the planet was being invaded by Martians. Just imagine having that kind of effect on people! When I went home later that evening, I asked my dad if he'd heard the radio play. He said that he hadn't, it was before his time. Not to be outdone, he went and got his copy of Jeff Wayne's *War of the Worlds*, the musical from the late 1970's, narrated by Richard Burton. I was absolutely gob smacked! That stayed with me for a while. These stories fired up my imagination.

Then there was John Wyndham, Richard E Matheson, Arthur C Clarke, William Gibson: the successors to Wells's great conceptual ideas. These giants of the literary world had their work adapted for the movies and television, the kind of work that's easily transferred onto the screen and radio. But it was Gibson and Matheson who blew me away with their ingenious ideas. To me, they *were* cinema! That was the inspiration, when you can 'see' a plot unfolding in front of your very eyes. When you can deduce elements of a radio play, a dialogue coming to life with such facilitation in your own mind.

I would talk to Sarah about them now and then to begin with. And after a while, as I went on about these writers and ideas quite a bit, she picked up on my enthusiasm and encouraged me to write my own. Yes, she really was very supportive. Even when I was talking shit or rabbiting on about nonsense, which was a lot of the time. I had written bits and pieces when I was younger, not all science fiction I might add. I even tried to write a kind of homage to Sherlock Holmes in honour of my grandfather. Unfortunately, it turned out to be farcical, so I just gave the other work to Sarah to look at. They were flash fiction rather than short stories.

Sarah read one or two of them. She was no fan of sci-fi herself, preferring to read non-fiction, mostly to do with art and philosophy which she still had a genuine passion for. But I have to say that Sarah did her best to encourage me from day one.

She said that my stories were quite interesting, if not quite juvenile. She said she could forgive me for that, because I was a man! Even so, I think it was the first time I had impressed her, other than by my surfing and swimming abilities. I sent the stories off to publishers and magazines - the usual thing for a naïve budding writer to do. They didn't get anywhere, so I decided to put the story-writing aside whilst I concentrated on studying again.

CHAPTER 2

I had never really been politically motivated, or idealistic in any way, until I started the master's course. I was studying comparative literature, and I soon had my eyes opened when I began to read Edward Said. His works were part of the compulsory reading for one of the modules. I would never have described myself as benighted in any way, but I definitely needed to be pointed in a certain direction when it came to learning. I knew very little about writers like Joseph Conrad, although I did know that *Apocalypse Now* was based on his novella *Heart of Darkness*.

Now I was delving into post-colonial novels and social realism, and that led to discovering Noam Chomsky, Raymond Williams, and Terry Eagleton. Big hitters of the intellectual left. I also read more about HG Wells, the Fabian society and his influence on social commentary in the English novel.

Sarah's father Tim also encouraged me to read Friedrich Hayek's *The Road to Serfdom*, and even Ayn Rand's far right meanderings, to get a sense of balance. It certainly enlightened and educated me in a broader sense, discovering how the world *really* works. Tim was a social democrat and a very fair-minded man, and he gave me some Harold Pinter and Arthur Miller plays to read. This was socially-conscious stuff that made a great impression on me. He was also informing me of the change of attitudes around the country, especially in working class areas like the North of England.

This was the most time that I had spent with Tim. I was enjoying his company, and he was clearly becoming a good influence on me. Around this time, the British public were due to vote in a referendum on whether to leave the European Union. I had admittedly been living in a comfortable little bubble with my family and the nice cottage by the coast, but now I started to take more notice of what was going on.

I went to visit my parents in Redcar for the first time in a while, and I could see that my parents were now struggling to stick to their political affiliations to the left. Anything other than a vote for Brexit was, it seemed, anathema to them.

It was nothing personal with my folks. We all got on well enough. It was just that I rarely got the chance to visit, with me being practically the other side of the country and all. But I knew they were very proud of my getting out, going to university, meeting Sarah, making that money off the flat, teaching. I didn't have any siblings either, so no-one to compete with for attention, I suppose. They were very down-to-earth and straight-forward people. My mother's family had lived in and around Redcar for many generations, but my father's father had moved down from Dundee after the war, to work in the steel works. He was a big union man there until his retirement.

My grandfather was also a self-educated man. Apart from Arthur Conan Doyle, he loved John Steinbeck. He read *The Grapes of Wrath* when he was a teenager and had wanted to be a writer. I once asked him why he hadn't, and he told me that his old school master had told him that to be a writer you needed imagination, talent, and intelligence. Then his teacher had added that my grandfather had none of those attributes. What a bastard! I swore then, that if I did go into education, then it would be in adult learning, to be able to give people that second chance.

My grandfather joined the army instead, just as the Second World War broke out. He ended up in Burma. He was one of the very few people who could drive in his regiment, so he transported tanks back and fore to the front on the back of a massive vehicle. I'd like to think that he would turn in his grave if he knew how things had turned out up there with the so called 'fall of the red wall'.

I decided to stay with my parents for a week, just to get more of a sense of what was happening up there. Sarah and I needed a break anyway. I had starting to get on her nerves lately, with all the studying, and now 'all of a sudden banging on about politics in the North' as she put it.

I had started to get these strange and unpleasant migraines. Quite debilitating to begin with, and they got worse quite quickly too. Another reason for staying was that my parents weren't getting any younger or healthier. My mother in particular had been worn down lately, after caring for her aunt and my grandmother, both of whom had recently passed away. Then she had the 'flu virus. Everything comes at once when you're on your knees, she said.

Her mood swings had started when I came up to see her and my dad about two years ago. Probably an age thing, I thought, although they both had arthritis too, and my mother was on and off steroid treatments. Back then, she was really pleased to see me. This time everything was up in the air. She was fussing around me one day, and I said that my visits had been too few and far between.

'Years have gone by since I was here last', I had said. Her whole persona suddenly changed, and she just replied,

'I wouldn't know son, I'm not a fucking calendar!'

During this short stay back home, I felt compelled to write an article on what I had been hearing and seeing in relation to a possible crisis on the horizon for the working classes and the traditional system of voting. Basically, shattered communities were being coerced into a rise in nationalism. Through an old mate of mine from university, I was able wrangle a meeting with one of the sub-editors of the local newspaper.

The article was clumsy and possibly naïve, but it must have hit a nerve. She was impressed by what she read, and it went into the paper's opinion column. From that piece, I was offered some freelance work with them. They also gave me the opportunity to spend some time in the offices, perhaps once a week. I was delighted, and so was Sarah. It gave her a break from my continuous waffling! It also meant that I could visit my parents' home more often as I had planned.

Being in the office gave me the opportunity to meet other members of staff. I soon became friendly with Richard, another journalist on the team. Apart from being a good reporter, he'd had two novels published. They had done quite well. Nothing to shout home about regarding sales, but from it he had received decent reviews, a good reputation locally, and more importantly an agent whom Richard trusted. He was reasonably impressed by my work and said that I was onto something. I just needed more depth - specifically more depth of character - if I was intent on being published.

The Master's course went well enough, and I graduated with mostly merits and a couple of distinctions. Standard stuff for a mature student I suppose. By now though, I was becoming more dedicated to writing the odd article for the paper, or fiction. Things were beginning to slowly work out, but still I whinged and moaned, as is my personality, along with being an obsessive, inquisitive dreamer. No, it wasn't enough. I had to get my stories published, even though I had only written a handful, and even though I had to admit that they were not that good. A hint of jealously kicked in as well: Richard had provided me with some competition. Friendly competition, but competition all the same. Maybe I was just deluded at that point. I wasn't exactly on his level, but I thought that I could be.

Again, Sarah was supportive, but unlike me, she was sensible. She warned me of pushing myself, that I didn't have anything to prove. She was becoming concerned about my mood swings that were due to the migraines, which had become more severe. I was travelling up to Redcar at least once a month now, and on two occasions, I'd had to pull over on the motorway for over half an hour due to my vision being impaired. I didn't want to admit to the obvious cause - that I was pushing myself physically and mentally.

These were strange migraines. Temporary sight loss, feeling confused and really nauseous, that kind of thing. So, I did the typical macho

31

thing, even though I wasn't a particularly macho type. Maybe more of that working class stoicism that was beginning to die with my generation. I carried on pretending that everything was fine, and that the migraines and the rest of it would pass. I just needed a good night sleep, that's all.

One November night, after a late meeting with my editor in Middlesbrough, I began to feel sick and nauseous again. I was also exhausted. I knew one of these awful migraines was coming on again. I phoned Sarah and told her how I was feeling. She immediately told me not to attempt to drive back to Padstow, but to get a room for the night, which I did. I pulled into a Travelodge on the outskirts of town.

I just about got to my room and put the card through the key slot. Then I closed the blinds before I crashed on the bed, but not before I hit the side of my head on a bedside cabinet.

'Fucking 'el,' I thought to myself, *'this is all I need!'*

God, this was the worst I had ever felt. It was like room-spin, nausea, a headache all in one go, followed by the vision impairment. It started off as it had done before, the left side of my vision was slowly but surely engulfed by the lines and shapes. I turned off the light. I had to. The light from the small lamp became a painful glow. Then I braced myself for the next half hour or so, prepared for partial sight loss, pain and confusion. This time, however, things took a different turn.

There was a great pressure all around my head, and I found it impossible to open my eyes. Not in the physical sense, but from this intensity that I was experiencing. Then the pressure lifted, just like a mist lifting from a valley floor. I suddenly found the lines and swirls filling the space in my mind and making distinct patterns. It was literally like a film projector, all of this in black and white lines and patterns. Before I knew it, shapes formed, actual faces, not faces that I could make out, but definitely faces, with blank expressions. There were two of them, facing opposite each other, like two posts either

33

side of a gateway. I felt as if I was in, or part of, another world filled with moving lines in black and white.

The two faces faded away, and then I saw these figures acting out a story-line in front of my eyes. I was startled, stunned even, but not frightened. It was like being in a trance. Hypnotised by my own mind. The figures and shapes were not exactly clear though, it was more like a poor TV reception. It also reminded me of something else, something I had seen in the past. Something quite primitive, something antique. Yes, a simple moving picture device, an old-fashioned film projector, that Sarah had written about for a portfolio back when we were studying. It had made an impression on me back then. These characters I was seeing continued to 'play out' these scenarios in front and around me for what seemed like hours.

The next thing I knew, it was the early hours of the morning. I had fallen asleep, but somehow, I remembered everything. Turning on the lights, I dashed into the ensuite bathroom to go to the toilet and wash. My vision was fine, and I looked okay, even though I was drained of energy. I went back into the room and turned on the television set.

The migraine - what in God's name was that? Was it a migraine? Were these spectres playing out my unconscious ideas? What had happened in here last night? I had bashed my head just before collapsing onto the bed, but it was nothing. I had a bit of a lump, and it felt slightly sore there on the side of my head, but what could constitute what had happened to me last night?! What's more, I remembered everything, every single part of that experience, performance, or maybe a 'journey' to somewhere else. Another part of my unconscious mind perhaps?

I took my laptop out of its case and sat by the desk. The words flowed out, flooded out. I couldn't write them quickly enough. All that I had seen, all that I had... imagined? I still wasn't completely sure at that point what it was that I had experienced. It took me about five hours all in all. Then I sat back and looked at it. There in front of me on the screen was a story.

A complete and coherent story! How the hell was I going to explain this to Sarah - or anyone else for that matter?

I checked out a couple of hours later, but not before I made a note of everything. My obsessive behaviour suddenly came rushing to the surface. I treated the place like a crime scene. I used my phone to take photos all around the room; walls, bed sheets, the cabinet that I banged my head on. It actually made me laugh as I was doing it. It must have been nerves, but I was aware of how ridiculous I must have looked. I made a note of the room number, the floor, pretty much everything.

Checking out, it suddenly came to me that yesterday was a Tuesday. I hated Tuesdays. Life caught up with me on Tuesdays. Every time I'd had a migraine, it had been on a Tuesday. Admittedly, none of the other migraines had delivered an experience like the one I'd gone through the previous night, but I started to become obsessed with Tuesdays. Why a Tuesday? I always felt like shit on a Tuesday, regardless of how my weekend had gone. But why any day in particular? I hated Tuesdays. Was there a connection?

CHAPTER 3

Well, no, it seemed there wasn't a connection at all. Because the next time I had one of these migraine-induced surreal experiences was a couple of weeks later, and it was on a typical, quiet Sunday afternoon back in Padstow.

On this particular day, Sarah had taken Lorna down to Newquay to do some Christmas shopping. I went for a long walk on the beach in the morning with the dogs, before I got onto some writing. I needed to finish an article for the newspaper, and I also wanted to look at the story from the night of my experience in my room in Middlesbrough.

The truth is, I was worried. Yes, worried, concerned even, but not frightened by the whole thing, as you'd imagine. I still hadn't mentioned anything to anyone, even Sarah. It was clearly brought on by stress, *a one-off event* I told myself. Unbelievable and incomprehensible, but a one-off. Surely? The sharp pains in the left side of my temple had not gone away. I'm sure that was neuralgia. A lot of my mother's side of the family suffered with that. Unpleasant, but nothing that I was particularly worried about.

So, I sat at my desk in the spare room and got to work finishing off the article. I had decided to write about the correlation between misinformation in the mainstream media and obesity. It didn't take me long to finish, just over an hour, but it wasn't particularly good either. Well, it was actually fucking rubbish, as you can imagine from the subject. Even I wasn't sure that there was a correlation to make an article work. The last two pieces I had written for them were only slightly better. I had lost my mojo. So, I allowed myself another hour to get my head together before I looked at what I had written out that morning after the strange migraine.

After a break playing around with the dogs in the garden, I went back up to the spare-room-cum-study and looked at that article again. It didn't read well this time either. In fact, it was pretty poor. I came to the conclusion that I was out of my depth here. I'd had a good 'spurt', but it seemed to be coming to an end.

It wasn't good news, because I needed to start providing for my family now. Sarah was still only working around 10 hours a week at this point. I didn't want to go back to tutoring either, and anyway, that was becoming more and more difficult to get into lately. My stories were getting nowhere, mainly because they weren't particularly good. I think Sarah had gone beyond her role of being the supportive partner as well. She was getting tired of it. She had been completely honest with me when I mentioned the stories I'd written, telling me that they were now just average at best.

I was getting despondent, which doesn't take much for me. The neuralgia was starting up again, that nasty tightness spreading down the left side of my head. The same area began to twitch and burn as well now. Tension and heaviness…Jesus, sounds like a fucking advert for Neurofen!

So anyway, I put my old memory stick into the side of my laptop and scrolled down the folders. There it was. *Migraine Story* I had titled it. I managed a slight chuckle. It just looked and sounded ridiculous. I clicked on it and had a look at what I had written. It turned out to be as complete and as coherent as I remembered from that morning I wrote it. It was the one that became *Stolen Goods*, the story I mentioned earlier about the inept burglars up in Middlesborough. Why, or more to the point how the hell would I write a story like that?! But there again, that's the point. I didn't actually *write* it.

I thought of the nights my dad would play me records from his teenage years. I wasn't particularly into music, never have been really. But my father, well, he was a dedicated Mod to begin with, a big Who fan. Then he got into softer stuff like country and western, especially Dolly Parton. I'm not sure why he went in that direction. Might have been her comically oversized breasts and her blonde hair, although he did like the melancholy lyrics of that style of music. Now and again after a few whiskeys he would attempt to sing one or two like, *No old*

41

flame can hold a candle to you, or *You ain't worth the salt in my tears.* Which one he chose depended on how well he and my mother were getting along at the time!

Yes, I remember him telling me that some of the great songwriters from that era would speak about 'receiving' songs, or song ideas. This was in the earlier days before hallucinogenic drugs, he hastened to add.

Well, I had certainly received something here. I re-read it again. It was so different, and far better than anything I had written before. It was in a different league, I was pretty sure of that. No, I'll be honest with you, I was absolutely certain of it! It was probably because what I was reading was not something that I had had to wrack my brains over for weeks, months even, trying to conceive and then execute those ideas in the usual fashion. No, I was actually reading something, a retelling of a tale that I had seen acted out in front of me during this debilitating and disturbing episode.

I couldn't stop reading over it and thinking about it. I had to stop at one point though, because the pain in the left side of my head was getting worse. I raced downstairs to let the dogs out to do their business, before racing back up the stairs to make sure everything was saved to my memory stick and the desktop. Just to make sure, I would also email myself this piece. Christ, it was really good! I was almost out of breath by the time I reached the room; I was dizzy with excitement and confusion. My mind was bombarded with possibilities. That's when it happened again.

My head began to spin and the nausea kicked in like it had done before. Stomach cramps, then the vision impairment, the lines and squiggles emerging from the left hand side. I remembered that my mother would refer to these as the 'zig zags'. Again, the heaviness from the top of my head downwards.

I struggled to keep my eyes open. *I really need to close the curtains and lie down*, I thought to myself. It was still light outside and Sarah would be back with Lorna from shopping soon. I stumbled across the room to close the curtains. *I want this to happen!* I was thinking. Then I just crashed onto the futon.

That immense pressure around my head again. It continued for some time, before the lifting of the mist. Then the lines - no, these *zig zags* - increased in size and density, more so than before, like a jagged-edged snake, swirling around what would be my peripheral vision. Like pieces missing in a jigsaw puzzle, the triangular, electrifying lines swirled round and round to form a ring, to become a circle...or a window? Then the faces, opposite each other, fading away to reveal figures, places, place names all forming in front of me again. The scene, a scene within a cylindrical shape, began to fill my mind's eye.

The whole thing reminded me of that old film projector apparatus again. I have to admit I was feeling anxious this time. Would it be the same outcome, the same scenario, the same ghostly characters coming out of this line-filled void? The images appeared, projecting even in that same fashion as the last time, but this time they seemed clearer. They were just like the

44

images inside that old film projection machine.

It was extraordinary, fantastical, but also frightening now. I felt myself falling into a window, or portal if you will. This time I just about managed to open my eyes slightly. The burning pain was still there. I looked down at my own arms, body legs. I was part of this freakish place, an out-of-body experience possibly? Confusion, but of course I was part of it. It was *my* fucking migraine…it was my fucking mind! If I hadn't been so scared, maybe it would have been more exhilarating.

Exhausted again by the experience, I fell asleep like last time. I was suddenly awoken by Lorna rushing into the room to see me. She grabbed her arms around me and asked me if I was unwell. I managed to tell her that I was fine, before kissing her on the forehead and giving her a hug. Then I said that I really needed to go to the bathroom. I did look okay, I think. I swilled my face, hands and neck and went back into the room. Lorna had gone downstairs. I slept, for only around an hour this time though.

And I felt light headed and queasy. Probably due to the shorter sleep, I thought.

As I continued to come to myself, it all came back to me again. The characters, the locations, the place names, the scenarios, the whole story! Then it struck me. There were two protagonists again. Why these two characters? why the two blank faces? I also realised that, as before, they played out situations which were unlike anything I could have written by myself. That mixture of the unconscious and my deepest imagination, pouring out into these episodes - or you could say 'adventures'.

I had to get all this down. What was I going to do this time? Sarah had just driven home for an hour with Lorna, I couldn't just sit there typing out this story again. She'd hit the roof. I had to make an excuse to go in the car, go for a drive, and literally talk this piece into my dictation recorder. I should have told Sarah at this point, obviously. But no, I told her that I had just spoken to her dad and that he needed me to pop round pronto to help him out with…something. She gave me a strange, slightly unconvinced look and said okay. Always so trusting...and forgiving.

I jumped in the car and called Sarah's dad and explained that I was on my way over. If Sarah called, just tell her that you had called me and really needed my help. He laughed, cheeky bastard. I took some beers over for him, made some excuse, and went into *his* spare room where I spent the next couple of hours quietly dictating my latest 'experience'.

So now I had these two stories. Longer, better and unlike anything I had produced before. Two very good stories in my own biased opinion. Ok, so I didn't actually write them, as *receive* them. At least I was being honest with myself, and I knew they were great. I just needed someone to take a look at them: I still needed that reassurance. Sarah and her dad were always honest with me, They would definitely be less biased than myself. They could look at them before I started taking them any further. I decided to get the holidays out of the way. January being such a miserable month, at least their opinions wouldn't be affected by the seasonal indulgences and jovialities.

I did exactly that. In the second week of a very cold, wet, miserable January, I asked Sarah and her father to have a good read of both stories. They were impressed, to say the least. Unsurprisingly, they both asked me how I had come up with such great work compared to my previous stuff.

'No offence of course,' they said.

'None taken!' I replied.

I didn't care, I was so pleased. I was onto something, from where, or from what recess of my own mind I didn't know, but I was…thankful. Well, thankful and bewildered.

I got in touch with Richard. I couldn't wait to tell him about these latest stories. I wished him a happy new year and all that nonsense, then I soon got onto the business of 'my latest work'. I liked Richard; he was honest with his opinions to the point of bluntness. That's a good thing when you're writing, though. Having smoke blown up your arse isn't going to improve your work or your chances of success.

When I mentioned how productive I'd been, he wasn't too keen at first. He was also taken aback by my enthusiasm. He had been good enough to take a look at my previous stuff, but he'd told me that it was lacking depth, definition etc.

I had read Richard's latest novel, and I had genuinely enjoyed it. We had similar interests when it came to literature and films, so I played on that quite a bit. I drilled home that these last couple of stories had a different feel.

'They're more like plays…cinematic you could say…perfect for the screen, just like your last book Richard…I think you may have inspired me!' I blurted out unashamedly.

So, after a pleasant enough conversation, he relented and asked me to send them up in an email. I did that immediately, and waited for his response. I also waited for my next migraine. It had been a few weeks since that last one.

In the meantime, I tried to write. 'Tried to write' being the appropriate phrase there, because nothing, literally nothing came to me. Not even shit stuff. Not even the poor quality rubbish that I would often put in for my English Literature A levels. At the same time though, I did turn in a couple of decent articles for the newspaper. That gave me the opportunity to see Richard again when I next visited the office.

I got in touch with him a couple of days before I was due to leave. Of course, he hadn't read any of my writing, not as much as a page. I was pissed off, but not really surprised. I laid it on thick about my dad not being so good, which was partly true. I said that I really needed him to have a look at what I'd sent him while I had the chance to take in any criticism clearly and calmly.

'Just read a chapter', I told him. 'These stories are longer than the other tales that I've written, but I'm sure you'll be into them.'

He agreed, and we arranged to meet for a few beers when I got there.

Over that next couple of days, before I left for my trip to the North, I thought long and hard about telling Sarah about what was going on. Obviously she knew that I had been suffering from these migraines lately, but she didn't have any idea what I was really going through. How could I convey to her what it was I was experiencing? She had always been an understanding person, but she was also the last person I could imagine who would believe in these crazy visions, or episodes, I was having. I was struggling to explain it all in the hypothetical conversations that I would have with her. I would have to say something eventually though, it was going to happen again, surely?

The day before I left, Tim asked me to go for a surf. It was now early February, and bloody cold! Cold, wet and miserable. Sarah had started getting into cold water swimming. It was becoming a craze with women over thirty then, middle class women to be precise. It was good for her though. She was still fit, and she loved a challenge. It also got her socialising again, which was good because I was going away almost once a week now. So Sarah's dad arranged for him, me and his mate to spend the morning surfing, before having a well-earned brunch.

The trouble is, I had forgotten just how fit Tim was. He was fifty eight then, but I swear that he must've been in the same condition as when he was a naval officer. He was a tough bastard, fair play. On top of that, his mate was like a younger, fitter versions of him. He was a barrister, very sure of himself. Don't get me wrong, I'd been almost, almost close to them at my peak, but lately I'd let myself go a bit. That Christmas didn't help either. I was still a strong swimmer, so I thought that I'd have a chance with his mate, but it turned out that he was a fitness fanatic, who practised martial arts. So, I turned up carrying a nice bit of excess weight, and the other two were in tip top condition.

But I didn't let it deter me from doing my unconvincing tough-northern-boy act. I probably put it on a bit much though, because the barrister from Devon started upping the pace. It was full on for the first hour or so. I knew that I was pushing myself to my limit, and even Sarah's dad dropped out. Of course, I had to keep it going. You know, not let the side down. I was out about forty metres or so when

I started to feel dizzy, then nauseous. Yes here it was, the 'next one', the migraine I had been waiting for…*hoping* for even, How fucked up does that sound! Hoping for a migraine episode! Only here I was, almost out to sea. I didn't want one of these episodes under these conditions, but then again, it wasn't a choice.

So now I'm slowly but surely losing my vision. I managed to make my way to the beach, before staggering on the sand, up towards my car with a fucking big surf board under my arm. By the time I reached my car, parked by the dunes, I could just about see. I heard Tim shouting up to me, asking if I was alright. I shouted back about having cramps or something, I can't actually remember to be honest. I tried to look and sound as together as possible, because I didn't want either of them to think that I was weak, especially the Kung Fu Barrister. I got into my car, clicked the seat back and waited.

The heaviness in and around my head was unbearable this time. Pressure like I had never felt. Was it down to being physically pushed to my limits? Whatever the reason, I was really starting to feel unwell. Again, what had been my vision started to become something else. Zig zags didn't form this time though. No. For whatever reason, swirling black and silver parallel lines took form. Then they unfolded, unravelled, from right to left now. Nothing happened for a while, then suddenly - the two blank faces. No other figures appeared. Just the same two blank faces either side, like a gateway. They reminded me of the statues on Easter Island - blank, expressionless, and 'squared off', not rounded. I say Easter Island, - I can only describe them in that way.

My memory of the 'event', along with the whole experience, was unlike the other times before or afterwards. They seemed to be pushing through the lines, like it was a sheet or a blanket, or when you slowly push your face underwater. It became like a whirlpool, jagged and electrifying. Yes, they were pushing towards me. Then they started to mouth words to me, somehow attempting to speak to me. God, this sounds so, so…insane to me now.

The pressure in my head continued to get worse. In fact, it was more intense than before. I felt as though I was going to pass out. There was no sign of it lessening, no sign of an idea, a concept or story, or, however you want to describe it, forming or happening either. Then suddenly this wall of parallel lines, with the blank faces, wrapped itself into that familiar cylindrical shape, the window that I was now used to seeing, before it began to fall away, downwards, into this void.

I put my arms out to follow it. As I did, I tried to speak back to the figures, although I didn't know what I was saying, or trying to say. It was as if I was unable to connect with them this time. At that point, the pressure in my head became unbearable. I felt a sharp pain in my temple like an electric shock, and then I passed out.

A knocking, that soon turned into a banging, brought me round. I looked up to see Tim and his mate staring at me from the window of the driver's seat. They both looked shocked. I opened the door, and they told me what they had seen as they approached the car. Apparently, I seemed to be in a trance-like state where my head was down on my chest, and my arms were raised shoulder level. It looked like I was trying to touch or grab something. That was obviously worrying enough. Then Tim quietly informed me that I was repeating nonsensical words over and over for a minute or so. In fact, he said that I had been speaking in tongues!

As I came to, I couldn't help but notice the look of concern and perplexity on Tim's face. The Kung Fu Barrister just stared at me like I was some kind of fucking alien life form. Couldn't blame him I suppose. The pain and exhaustion was greater than I had felt before. On top of that, I felt really embarrassed. I gestured to Tim to come closer to me so that I could quietly speak to him. I pleaded with him not to mention anything to Sarah.

I have already mentioned that Tim had always been fair minded and understanding, maybe too understanding. He knew deep down that I wasn't really good enough for his daughter. Sarah was really special, she had everything to offer and more. Still, he did his best to support us both, as a couple and individually. He promised that he wouldn't repeat anything to Sarah about what he had seen me going through, but also made me promise that I would seek medical help as soon as I could. I managed to mumble something about an important meeting coming up that I just couldn't afford to miss, regardless of my condition. Some bullshit like that anyway.

To this day, I wish that he had told Sarah. Then none of this would have turned out like it did. I was acting so selfishly, but I was also very confused, and now very worried, as you can imagine.

CHAPTER 4

Two days later, I went up to meet with Richard. As much as I was anxious about what I was experiencing, I have to admit that the excitement of finding out from him what he thought of my 'work' just drove me on.

We met for dinner and some drinks in a bar just across the road from the offices. Richard didn't hesitate to tell me that he was really bowled over by the stories, or the 'unusual, but interesting tales' that I had given him. Just like Sarah and her father had said before him, Richard had to make a point of telling me that this new stuff was in another stratosphere to the other work I had given him in the past. I told him with a smirk that I was pretty much expecting him to say something like that.

As we ordered our drinks, he opened his lap top up, there and then, and pulled up the word docs I had mailed him. I was taken aback by his enthusiasm, even though I knew that I was going to make an impression on him. Then he began to point out sections and pieces of the stories, how great they were, how I'd captured the depth that I had been lacking in my previous writing, how I had 'grasped the art of storytelling'. He enthused that he could see everything playing out in front of him. *'Funny that you should say that!'* I thought to myself.

Before I could interrupt him with a courteous 'thank you', he became really excited about the…hold on, let me get his words right: it was the 'depictions of magical realism you have contributed to your concepts and characters'. I blurted out something about Bertolt Brecht, to which Richard quietly informed me that Brecht was more about the 'theatre and absurdity, or rather the Epic Theatre'. That made me feel like a right tit.

'There are also snippets of Dadaism in there,' he said.

I didn't even respond to that. He followed up with the tales being more reminiscent of Borges' Labyrinths.

'Right Richard, of course they are. I was hoping that you would notice that,' I replied.

It was dishonest of me, but what did I care? My worries about my condition were now at the back of my mind. Richard did love his terminology. He then went on to talk about what struck him most, like the 'dialectics between the two protagonists', and the 'surreal, yet dramatic situations I had created'.

This was fantastic: to hear someone I admired as a writer, a published and respected author, going on like that to me. 'Created' he'd said! Well, I had to suppress a childish giggle on that comment. If only he knew! He did imply at one point that this latest work of mine was *so* good, that maybe, just maybe I had found my inspiration from someone else. I just asked him straight out at this point that he wasn't referring to me indulging in plagiarism. There was a very brief pause, of awkward silence before he shook his head. Then he told me that he was going to put the story forward to Jane Lilly. Jane was a respected London-based agent from Newcastle who had strong links with the television and theatre industry in the north of England.

Richard half-jokingly admitted that it pained him to this, just in case he was shooting himself in the foot. Apparently, she had recently put forward one of Richard's own scripts for a one-off television drama. I mean, Jesus, this really was great new! This *was* a gift horse surely? One with its mouth wide open, it would appear. I admired Richard. Not just as a writer and as a professional, but also as a person. He was a straightforward and sensible man. Furthermore, he had always been upfront and honest with me. I was delighted, to say the least. So much so, that I went into sycophantic mode with him. Yes, I can play the creep if I have to. Well, how else do you get on in this life?

At the end of our fruitful conversation, Richard gave me some advice about how to deal with any potential contact with Jane, or someone else from the agency. He told me to be ready to drop everything if they do ask for a meeting.

'Chances like these are very few and far between, so don't blow it!', he said.

He went on to say that he thought I was in with a good chance of getting work produced here, especially with what I now had to offer. Who was I to argue? I took his advice on board, thanked him for everything, and went back to my hotel. Oh, one other thing: I had to look up the subject and theory of magical realism in literature. I was ashamed to admit to myself that I knew very little about it, just the basics about Salman Rushdie and Gabriel Garcia Marquez. I had no idea about the film productions, so how would I be able to speak at length in a potential meeting about how my 'work' was apparently reminiscent of this particular style? Apart from that, the social commentaries were obviously going to be easier to explain. Oh, I also read up a bit on Borges and his 'labyrinths'.

I remember calling Sarah as soon as I got back to my hotel. She was obviously pleased for me, but she also told me to keep my feet on the ground. Level-headed advice as usual from her. It was clear that Tim hadn't mentioned anything to her about that incident at the beach, but I had a feeling I would have to explain to her what was going on at some point.

It was an uneventful night at the hotel, nothing like the last time I had stayed up here in the Travelodge. My mind flipped between what had happened since that first disturbance, and what all this might lead to: an unexplained, and certainly unexpected, helping hand onto what seemed to be the road to success. I didn't want to spend the foreseeable future getting on Sarah's nerves just waiting around in a stupor for that possible all important call from Jane Lilley, or even one of her minions.

As I was about to leave my room the next morning, I had a call from Liz, the sub-editor at the paper. My first article for them had gained quite substantial interest online since the Brexit result. Could I come up with a follow-up article, something good, and pronto? I jumped at the chance.

I have to admit that it wasn't the most difficult thing that I'd ever written. The initial article was the whole basis for this one. I made it more of a retrospective work than anything else. I was being a bit lazy, but I knew that they would print it. It was good enough anyway, and it would provide me with some much-needed income.

After that work, it was looking like I would have to get a teaching position if the agency didn't get back to me. It had been two months since my meeting with Richard, and I still hadn't heard anything. I had to resist calling them a few times. I knew that would be a mistake, and Sarah and her dad were telling me to hold my nerve and be positive.

Good old Tim had still kept his word - he hadn't told Sarah about my episode at the beach, although he did approach me, in secret, to ask if I had spoken to a doctor.

'It was pretty disturbing, seeing you like that,' he said to me.

Not half as disturbing as experiencing it, I thought to myself. Nevertheless, I did promise him that I would see someone about what was going on with me. He had kept his promise after all. More to the point, he was very concerned, and shocked, that I was actually keeping all this from Sarah, and apparently not doing anything about it. I just couldn't explain to him then everything that was happening - the visions, or adventures…or whatever the fuck I could call them. *That* was the reason I wasn't telling Sarah - my wife, his daughter - or anyone else for that matter. Apart from that, I hadn't experienced anything since that time anyway. Nothing. Not even a bit of a headache.

I heard nothing for another couple of weeks after that. Reluctantly, I started to look for supply-teaching work. That was quite depressing after my initial euphoria following the meeting with Richard. Then, out of the blue, I received a phone call from Jane Lilley herself. She was calling from her second home in Malta. After a brief introduction, she went straight into the potential of *Stolen Goods* as a radio play, possibly even a screen play. I looked across the room at Sarah, and excitedly mouthed the words, *'fucking hell…Jane Lilly…radio…screen play…'* to her. She smiled and blew me a kiss. I remember that well.

65

Then Jane spoke about Richard, and how much respect she had for him.

'He speaks so well of you, and of your latest work of course.'

I told her how pleased I was to hear that, and that I couldn't speak highly enough of him myself...especially after this! She also mentioned how she was hoping to put Richard's last book forward for a series, but things were getting very competitive, what with the growth of streaming services, and the number of new writers such as myself producing great ideas. Thanks Jane! Then she spoke to me about the 'social conflicts represented in your work...the world is in so much turmoil...so much inequality my dear..'.

'I doubt if you see much of that in your luxury Maltese villa,' I found myself thinking. She was dropping a few 'darlings' into the conversation, and there was no trace of a Geordie accent from her. But why would there be? Her father had been a successful music promoter back in the 'seventies and 'eighties. A right tyrant, I've since discovered. She had only

known the world of wealth and fame. There again, my own native 'Smoggy' accent had been well watered down, if not completely dropped by the end of my first year at university.

I was picturing the scene on the other side of the telephone line: some actors and producers hanging about in the background, eating fancy expensive nibbles and drinking top-notch booze in the scorching Maltese sun. Of course, I was picturing myself and Sarah amongst them as well…yep, such a hypocrite.

Jane asked me if I had more work of this quality lined up. I lied and said that I did. Yes, I would worry about that later. Because something was going to turn up for me surely? Then she echoed Richard's comments on the magical realism influence. Oh, I'm prepared for this subject now, I thought. My mind swiftly went back to the conversation. Let's hear what you've got to say about it then. She started to blow smoke up my arse.

'The whole *Surrealism* thing…the French will love it you know...how you have taken such a mundane subject and turned it into such a fantastical adventure. I think that with the right director and cast on board, *Stolen Goods* and even your other story, *Going Somewhere?*, has the potential to stand alongside some wonderful magical realism film....*Big Fish, Perfume*, and even Lass Hallstrom's *Chocolat.*'

I was so excited and nervous that I tried to make a joke about that last sentence sounding like a Marks and Spencers' shopping list...God, the ignorance! I sounded like a right tit again, just as I had with Richard.

'Please ignore that last comment, Jane,' I said, embarrassed

'What comment?' she asked. Fortunately, she hadn't heard me, what with all that commotion in the background.

Well, at least the cinematic aspect of the stories was my own idea, along with the actual titles. I had *that* much input! It seemed that science fiction was a thing of the past now. I wasn't experiencing that kind of concept so far. Anyway, she said that she was staying out in Malta for both business and pleasure for a while, so one of her staff would be in touch over the next few days to arrange a meeting with regards to a contract and future dealings. I was beside myself with joy.

Sarah and I travelled to London the following week, where I had that meeting to negotiate my contract with Jane. It also gave us a chance to have a much-needed weekend away. Both the agency's and my solicitor were present. They offered me a thirty five thousand pound advance based on the two ideas that I had already given them. The agency would get fifteen per cent of my further earnings in book form, as well as radio and television royalties. I also had to provide them with another four concepts, stories, or scripts over the next twelve months.

That's when the reality kicks in. It's no longer about your time now, you're contracted to a company that's expecting you to produce work of a good standard and within a set timeframe. Ok, so this was it. It was an opportunity that I and thousands of other writers were searching for. I still only had *Stolen Goods* and *Going Somewhere?* at this point though. I knew that I couldn't possibly write anything on the same level on any given day. Although it had only been just over a year since that first occurrence in the motel, and a few months since the beach incident, who knows what was to come? A deadline would help to keep me focussed and occupied, I thought. It might also help bring on something else...like another creative 'helping hand'.

I was equally excited and worried over the following weeks. Meanwhile I thought I would treat myself to a luxury garden office, or *The Writing Shed*, as we named it. Five grand it cost. I saw one advertised in *The Times Literary Supplement* (Yes, I was reading that now), and thought that it was just what a professional writer needed. I had plenty of time on my hands, but no ideas forthcoming. I could see this glorified garden shed being filled with boxes of crap soon. Sarah and her dad took the piss out of me something awful. They called me all the pretentious bastards going. It also pissed Sarah off because I was wasting money already. They were obviously dead right.

Around that time, Lorna had been off school with a heavy cold. I was doing my best to look after her and the two dogs, because Sarah had been helping her friend run her arts and craft stall. I decided to have a belated celebratory bash with Tim and Sarah one evening. I wanted to thank them both for their support, and I was planning on somehow explaining what was going on to the two of them. Well, Tim was obviously aware of something, and it wasn't fair on him to keep it from his daughter anymore. Sarah came home in the early evening with her dad in tow. I had spent most of the day doing my daily chores, tending to Lorna and still trying to do my best to come up with some form of a creative idea. I had also opted to cook, rather than get a takeaway.

By the time we had all sat down for the meal, I'd had my fair share of wine. I started to feel dizzy, unwell. Need I explain what came next? I muttered that I was feeling nauseous, and that maybe I had better go upstairs. Probably the wine, I said. Sarah got up and asked me if I was going to have one of those terrible migraines again. I noticed Tim looking at me with an alarmed expression. I mumbled something about needing to lie down, before making my way upstairs. I was already losing my vision. Sarah began to follow me, but I told her to stay with Tim and Lorna, and that I would be fine after a rest.

I was rapidly losing my balance as well as my sight now. I staggered just like the other times into our bedroom. Although it was already dark outside, I closed the curtains, more through habit than anything else, although maybe, subconsciously, I didn't want interference of any kind. That expected pressure began, pulsing down from the top of my head. It was almost unbearable as before. I had to place a hand each side of my head in an attempt for comfort, although I knew nothing was going to alleviate this tension. I had to press my eyes hard now, and just wait for the zig zags, and the lines, shapes, swirls and faces...or whatever it was that might pre-empt another experience.

I managed to stay calm. I was thinking, *'will I find something, see something this time? ...receive some concept?'*. But it was just like the last time at the beach. The same two blank, expressionless faces. Pushing towards me like faces rising from water, from a whirlpool of swirls and jagged lines, then slowly falling back again, but slower this time. I briefly had the feeling of a warm sensation passing over me, like I was being enveloped by the whirlpool's edge. Then, as before, I seem to remember trying to speak to them, to connect, or make contact. Afterwards I wondered whether it was a case of me, or 'them', being unable to make a connection. A sharp pain, like a bolt of lightning, shot down my left temple. That's the last thing I remember about that disturbance, because I must have passed out, or fallen asleep again.   This time when I came to, Sarah was sat at the foot of the bed, and Tim was stood over her. A lamp was on in the corner. I was still in a state of confusion when I managed to look up at them both. Even then I could see that they looked horrified. My trousers and the bed sheets were soaking wet. I had pissed myself. That must have been the warm feeling at the whirlpool's edge that I had experienced. Or was it the wine taking affect?

Apart from soiling myself, I had apparently been grabbing at the air for a few moments. Like before, I had also been speaking out loud. I had been repeating, *'I can't connect with you…I can't connect with you!'* before babbling away in a strange, monotonal way. 'Speaking in tongues', as Tim had previously described it. Only this time, both he and Sarah were present.

It was obviously a terrible shock to Sarah; at least Tim had witnessed it before. They waited for me to come round properly before Sarah asked what the hell was happening to me. During my 'altered state', Tim had kept her calm, and persuaded her not to go too near me in case something else happened. He had also explained to her about the time at the beach, and the promise not to say anything to her. He told her that we had agreed not to mention it then, because neither of us wanted to worry her. Well, it was all out in the open now.

When I did come round, properly, the three of us went back downstairs. Understandably, they had put Lorna to bed when they had heard the strange noise coming from the bedroom. This time I had only been in that state for around a half hour. That was about the same length of time that I used to experience migraines before the other things came with them. Was I going back to that, I thought? Just common everyday health problems? Tim offered to stay, but Sarah said it was fine, that there was no need. We both sat at the dining table, with the uneaten food still on their plates. Before I could explain myself, Sarah gave me a quiet interrogation: How long had I been having these experiences?...Had the migraines always been that way?...Why hadn't I told her sooner?...Did my parents know?...Had I actually spoken to *anyone* about it all?

I calmly explained everything to her. How, when, where, what it was exactly that I had been going through. I was surprised how well she was taking it. Well, it wasn't as if I had been unfaithful to her. I had just kept this from her till now, because it sounded so fucking strange! The hardest part was convincing her that these ideas and concepts that had got me this deal all stemmed from these migraine episodes. She struggled to comprehend it, even though there was an obvious and distinct improvement in the quality of my writing since these experiences. But now it seemed like I was just freaking out.

I described to her how the ideas were formed: the swirls, lines, faces…everything. I said something about an old *Who* LP my father had. The mad drummer, Keith Moon - he had a T shirt on with this…design, these swirls. That's as close as I could come to describing it. Sarah told me that was a design by Bridget Riley, a famous pop artist, before getting out one of her books on modern art. There it was, the swirling lines and circles, classic sixties era designs. A *vortex!* That was it, that was the word I was trying to find to describe the experience. Just like the image on Keith Moon's top. It was very similar, I had to admit. Sarah looked at me, concerned.

Then I told her about the projector thing, that cylinder forming in my mind's eye the first couple of times, the times when the stories seemed to play out before me.

'I remember you writing about it back in the day, in one of your college portfolios,' I said to her.

She hesitated for a moment or two. I mean, you can imagine how strange and worrying this must have all sounded to her. Apart from that, she had just seen her husband pissing the bed and talking in tongues before her very eyes! Nice stuff. After another moment of quiet contemplation, she got a different book from the shelves and found a page. She came to a page with some illustrations and a description of a Zoetrope. She handed me the book, and I read it out.

'*A Zoetrope is a device, or optical toy that produces the illusion of motion from a rapid succession of static pictures....a cylinder has slits cut vertically on its sides...on the inner surface of the cylinder is a band with images from a set of sequenced pictures…'* It felt like one had been stuck in my head.

What had changed? Why were these last two experiences different to the first two? Was it the exercise, or the alcohol? Or maybe it was because on those times I had been alone. I didn't have a clue really. How the hell could I possibly know? I explained to Sarah that I hadn't scoured the search engines at any point or thought about any repercussions in my life because I was worried that I had developed a serious condition, and bizarrely, I didn't want to 'lose' this strange creative succour that I had received, these 'helping hands' if you will. I didn't want to get into a spiral of self-diagnosis either.

Now, more importantly, I had gained this lifeline, this great opportunity through Richard, and then. more importantly, Jane Lilly. Under normal circumstances, I would have been filling my trousers, not wetting them. I certainly would have spoken to Sarah from the outset, and no doubt sought professional help. I say 'normal circumstances': what the hell was normal about any part of all this, and what is 'normal' anyway? Well, it's clearly not having to go through these experiences.

I was suffering all this because I had gained so much to begin with. Now, for whatever reason, something else was happening. I agreed with Sarah that I would seek help the very next day, although it was still with some reluctance, I must say.

CHAPTER 5

Both Sarah and I had private health insurance, so I was able to organise an appointment with a specialist neurologist quite quickly. We also decided that it would be a good idea to see someone based close to my folks. It had been a while since we had visited them with Lorna. That would please them for sure.

Due to a cancellation, I was able to make an appointment for the following week. It was with a lady named Dr Phillipa Marshall. She had an excellent resumé and was fully accredited to three renowned private health clinics across England. My appointment with her would be in Leeds. Sarah had also encouraged me to look up any information related to migraine disorders and creativity. That seemed such an obvious thing to do, but I had been lacking any form of 'obviousness' throughout my adult life.

A couple of days before we were due to leave for my appointment, I took my lap top into the almost-redundant garden office, and began to look up anything I could find on migraines and creativity. I didn't really have my hopes up as I sipped my coffee (decaffeinated on Sarah's strict orders), and looked out onto the sodden patio. The rain was belting down - it was a gloomy April day. Here I was, about to do some random, and probably hopeless, internet search, if not to please my wife, then to convince myself that I wasn't cracking up, or had some kind of unwanted growth making its home in my head...or even both.

My initial trepidation soon turned into astonishment when I saw the results of my search. It was there in front of me: articles and essays on the theories and positive sides to migraines being linked to creative inspiration and ingenuity. Theories attributing the inventive imaginings of *Alice in Wonderland* to migraine phenomena being experienced by Lewis Carroll. This was just incredible. I couldn't believe what I was reading. The line:

'You suddenly think you're very short or you're very tall..', was apparently taken directly from one of Carroll's episodes. There was even a quote from a documentary made about the creative by-product of the condition:

'Alice In Wonderland has so many migraine moments in it I wouldn't know where to start...'

And this was just the first thing I came across! I read on...

'Migraines are also thought to have fuelled creativity in figures including Sigmund Freud, Georgia O'Keeffe, Virginia Woolf... and even Thomas Jefferson ... they're more common in children than you might expect ...'

One doctor in the film notes that: *'headache is the third-most-common symptom in kids coming to the Emergency Department, many of whom suddenly showing gifts or talents that they had previously not had...'.*

Other articles spoke of patients leaving notes for themselves with complex mathematical formulae on their fridge doors, for Christ's sake. These people either had no, or very little, previous knowledge of formulae to begin with, never mind not remembering how or why they wrote them! Another case told of a woman who would awaken from a migraine-induced deep sleep to find graphic drawings of wild animals on pieces of paper covering the floor. She also had no previous artistic training or skills. At least I had some background in writing.

Jesus! I mean…where did I start with all of these incredible facts and information?! It was all there, on the screen, for anyone to see. It still is, you don't have to take my word for it. Look for yourselves. I did notice that there was no mention of speaking in tongues or incontinence though. There again, even I wasn't stupid and naïve enough to think that all these individuals had lived through the same disturbances and events as me.

What it did mean, though, was that I clearly wasn't alone in my experiences. I now had some kind of an idea, knowledge even, of what was going on, of what I was going through. I also had this information to speak with Dr Marshall about at my appointment.

We drove up to Leeds the afternoon before my appointment. Well, Sarah drove to be precise. She was concerned about me being in control of the car, just in case. It was a fair and sensible thing to do, but it made me realise just how serious this condition was now. Sarah, Lorna and I stayed overnight in a nice hotel just outside the city centre. We had some great food and just a couple of glasses of wine to unwind. My appointment was at ten the next morning. The clinic was a twenty minute drive from the hotel, travel permitting.

The next morning, I was waiting anxiously in the reception area of the clinic. Sarah was pretty calm as usual, and Lorna played a game on her phone. The second movement of Beethoven's Moonlight sonata, the well-known bit, was playing quietly over the speakers. It did help to sooth my nerves, I must admit. I was called at 10am on the dot and made my way alone to Dr Marshall's room.

Although it was irrelevant to my treatment, she was nothing like I expected her to be. For some reason I was expecting a robust, Germanic looking woman. However, when she greeted me, I was struck by how tiny she was. She was like a sparrow, a bespectacled sparrow in fact.

This is going to sound really daft, pathetic even, but to begin with I found it hard to take her seriously. She asked me to take a seat, then she sat directly opposite me. My mind began to wander, as it often does, especially in stressful situations such as this. Sat on that big, padded chair with her legs unable to touch the ground, she reminded me of Ronnie Corbett during his famous monologues, or even Kermit the frog when his legs would dangle off the stage mid song. Oh well, at least these daft thoughts helped put me at ease for a bit.

The room was exactly what I was expecting though - you know, that typical interior of a practitioner's room: white walls, a desk, the two chairs, a shelf full of medical journals and books, a couple of strategically placed plants, a family portrait on the desk, and a print on the wall. I think it was a cubist painting. Sarah would have known. There was a large diagram of a dissected human brain on the opposite wall. Lovely. The blinds were partly closed, but there was still a decent view of the maintained gardens outside. Oh, and the sun was out for a change. Thank you, sunny Leeds.

I remember more about the details of the room than anything else to be honest with you, which is strange. But this is a strange tale, about a strange man. Anyway, Dr Marshall did her best to help me relax whilst I explained as much as I could to her about my experiences. I told her about how they had begun as just typical but unpleasant migraine conditions: the pressure, the neuralgia that accompanied them, the tension, sight impairment.

Then I went on to describe what was clearly not regarded as being quite as typical: the sight impairment turning into sight loss, turning into lines, swirling lines, vortexes, electrifying objects, faces, figures, figures acting out adventures to be more precise. Somewhere along the way, I mentioned reading about Lewis Carroll, Virginia Wolfe, and some of the other people in those articles online, if only just to make myself sound less mad!

Then I spoke of the Zoetrope thing, the way the images were 'projected', then the Keith Moon T shirt...or the Bridget Riley design. I reluctantly told her about pissing myself, and about 'grabbing the air', and talking in tongues, and Sarah not letting me drive anymore ... all that I could think of. Every last detail. Fuck it, it had to be done.

I felt like I was talking in tongues at that moment ... the words were flying out from my mouth before I could think about what I was saying. Dr Marshall just sat there looking at me. Well, looking at me and taking notes. I doubt if she would have had a chance to get a word in even if she had tried! I almost brought on a migraine there and then, which is understandable when you think about the circumstances.

Finally, I managed to explain to her the whole situation with Jane Lilly, and how it seemed that I was no longer 'receiving concepts'. Even though I had only just read about these incredible experiences other people with migraines had gone through, I still expected her to either piss herself laughing, or call the authorities ... or both. She did neither. She just sat there quietly her notes, before she gave me her verdict.

She spoke slowly, and with authority. This was definitely a good thing. If her voice had befitted her miniature, almost comical appearance, then I don't think the rest of the appointment would have gone particularly well. It was soon clear to me that she was a consummate professional, as you would expect from an established clinical neurologist. She first asked me about my background, about my family, any accidents that I had suffered in the past, any trauma etc. She asked about my childhood, my upbringing and my parents, school, university, then onto work and family, stress issues, psychiatric disorders and all that.

She then went into detail about the probable causes of my migraines, which were obviously stress and tension in my case. These are common causes. Following that, she brought up the hereditary nature of the condition, to which I was able to say that my mother had suffered with migraines. I hastened to add that as far as I was aware, she had never experienced anything like I had. There again, I hadn't really discussed what I had been experiencing with anyone until now. Apart from that, my mother was a very simple, straight-forward woman. She liked her needlework projects, baking, and her daily fix of soap operas.

'Your wife was right not to let you drive for the time being,' she said.

I told her that Sarah had always been the sensible, rational-thinking one in the relationship. Dr Marshall then made it plain to me that she didn't want me to drive, or undertake any task that may involve risk, before I started taking something for the migraines. She finished by informing me that I would have to undergo an electroencephalogram (EEG), which would measure my brain waves. It was just a case of placing electrodes, which are small metal discs, on my scalp. By doing this, Dr Marshall would be able to scan my brain activity to see if the causes were from pain, a brain disorder, brain damage, brain dysfunction, or a tumour. I was fine with this. What I really wanted to hear from her was - what the hell was happening with these 'other things'? I didn't know how else to put it.

Dr Marshall conducted the scan straight away. While her tiny hands were busy placing the small metal discs around my scalp, I began to convince myself that there would be some kind of abnormality, like a growth, something malignant. How else would I be going through this in the first place?! However, the scan was fine. Dr Marshall told me to sit back down and she returned to her own seat. She put her notes down onto the desk, and placed her childlike hands onto her lap, before she did her best to try and explain to me what it was that I might be experiencing.

The more common aspects of my condition, like the visual impairment, Dr Marshall referred to as 'visual snow'. Ok, that sounded better than 'zig zags'. She spoke about the twitching and the neuralgia, the dizziness, heaviness in limbs, just about everything I had gone through. She told me that all these symptoms were fairly common, and quite easily treatable.

However, there was a pause before she began to address the more unusual and weird symptoms that I had gone on to suffer. I was taken aback when she mentioned the term 'Glossolalia' to describe the speaking in tongues incident. So, it was actually 'a thing'? Apparently, there were two forms: 'Static', where the individual repeats the same thing over and over, and 'Free-Association', where words are spoken in free form. From what Sarah and her father had told me, I fell into the latter category.

Yes, it was a 'non-neurogenic language disorder' (I made her write the terms down for me by the way), and not a neuro-psychiatric disorder. Although she did say that in this case, the trauma of the experiences was probably triggering it. That would also explain the incontinence as well. I was already cringing at the thought of having to buy myself some incontinence pants in the future.

Well, that was a start, but what about the faces, the vortex thing … the stories? This is where it got complicated. The first thing Dr Marshall spoke about was a phenomenon called 'Pareidolia'. I hadn't heard the actual scientific term, but I knew what this was. It was basically when someone sees faces in inanimate, natural objects, like the outline of a face in a cloud, or on the surface of the moon, or Mars etc. Like the photos from alien conspiracy documentaries and so forth. Only some people experience this phenomenon on a regular, even daily basis.

Dr Marshall almost lost my confidence at this point. She was basically trying to say that the initial 'visual snow' and 'brain fog' (this is another symptom where your mind goes into a sort of slowing down or shutting down process) that I was experiencing at the start of my migraines was possibly leading to great confusion and also this Pareidolia, and that's where the faces and figures seemed to appear.

I wasn't convinced by this, and I made it plain to her that what I was experiencing was something different to this, something internal, something even more bizarre, and, lately, frightening. I knew *that* much!

This led her to another possible, or more probable explanation. At this point, her voice became slightly louder, and even more authoritative, like she was giving a speech. She explained that neurology and physiological studies obviously overlap in some circumstances such as mine. A bit of a lecture followed on studies of the unconscious mind by some of the great thinkers in modern times such as Descartes, Hursserl, Heidegger, Sartre and of course Freud. She flicked through her notes for a brief moment, as I waited anxiously for what was coming next. She told me that the cases I had spoken of, where people have performed things, tasks, so forth using skills and talents that they were unaware that they had or were unsure that they could perform to that extent, that was a form of 'depersonalisation', Lewis Carroll being the most famous case.

It was a rare and severe symptom relating to migraines, that was more common in mental illness. With mental illness, the term was used to describe unpleasant feelings of strangeness, as if you are outside your body, being watched, losing control and so forth. Dr Marshall was keen to emphasise that in the case of some migraine sufferers, this particular form of depersonalisation appeared to 'open up' areas of the unconscious mind in an almost psychedelic sense, rather than being related to actual personality disorders. I told her about the 'magical realism' situations that people were referring to in my writing, which I had to admit was quite alien to me. She replied that this was a good case in point.

'Your experiences are so surreal, this is how they are interpreted into your ... work.'

I was still struggling to take all this complex information in, as she carried on in a matter-of-fact way. She went on to inform me that the changes in the experiences, or episodes, could be an underlying fear of failure, crossing over once again from the unconscious mind, just like the creative visions, although these came from a darker recess, a deepening of the imagination. I couldn't help but think to myself, *'Was that my creative Mr Hyde?'*

She ended by telling me that these conditions are more involved in neuropsychology.

'What we can be sure of, though, is that your condition, the migraine, is at the core of all these symptoms, both those that are common, and those that are, as you say, bizarre. So that's where the treatment must begin *and* end. That's where we'll put a lid on things. Put a lid on what is clearly becoming a very worrying and debilitating condition.'

I mentioned the deal with Jane Lilly again, apprehensive now, and my worry that I wasn't going to able to provide her with any further worthwhile material, '...not without - ...a helping hand...' Dr Marshall looked at me with disapproval.

'Well in your case, what is more important to you? Your wife and family and your health, or chasing success and impressing people?'

Hearing her say that to me…I just stared at the floor in shame. She wrote me a prescription and gave me a follow-up appointment for the following month. And that was it, my hour was up.

CHAPTER 6

We drove straight to my parents' home after that. It was quiet, but not unpleasant in the car. The eighty mile journey seemed to pass quickly, for me anyway. In my head, I was still back in Dr Marshall's room. I was trying my best to engage with Sarah; Lorna was continuing with her game in the back seat.

Sarah asked me the questions that I was expecting: What was said? What was she like? Did I tell her everything? Did I get any answers? What happens now? I went over everything with her as best as I could: what the strange symptoms could possibly be, the causes, the scan, the medication, and so on. I didn't mention the Jane Lilly thing.

It took us just under two hours to get to Redcar. My folks were delighted to see Sarah and Lorna ... and me of course. They were proud of my achievements with the publishing deal and the stories. Both Mum and Dad looked well, and they had clearly brushed up for the occasion. We had already decided to stay until

Sunday, so that the drive back for Sarah would be easier.

It was such a treat, seeing the fuss they made, especially over Lorna. She rarely got the chance to see them. She was almost ten years old now, and the image of her mother. I think my parents were secretly glad of this, because I had never been particularly attractive. Like most men, my father was smitten with Sarah from day one. She had the personality and the charm, as well as the beauty.

My mother thought the world of her too. She often alluded to me as 'punching above my weight' on occasions like these. My dad would just shrug his shoulders, but I knew that he thought the same way. Like most people, I suppose. Sarah was shocked when I first told her about this, but I said that it was just how they had been brought up. They were well into their thirties when they had me, their only child. No room for snowflakes back in their day, I would say to her.

They were a taciturn pair, but when they fell out, boy did they fall out! I used to have

Sarah in stiches when we first started seeing each other, recounting the arguments they would have when I was a kid. It would go on for days, I told her. It was true. I remember times when they would sit in their chairs in the front room, in front of the television. The sound would be on low, and then they would start.

My mother would usually start the proceedings by calling my dad a creep, and then my dad would answer back by calling her a liar. *Creep, liar...creep, liar...*and so forth. Yes, on it would go. It was funny and worrying at the same time, especially when it went on for days at a time. Fortunately, they would always make up. Then everything would be forgotten between the two of them, and they would go to the social club for a good old fashioned sing song.

Whenever we did visit them, after a few drinks at home, they would always go on about their courting years. The days spent hanging around the pier, then as they got older, the nights spent in the clubs in Redcar and

Middlesbrough. Places like the Top Deck, the Starlight., and Bongos.

'Cheap beer, and even cheaper women!' my father would chirp.

Then my mother would give him that look, and he'd soon start talking about how they would enjoy their Parmos on the way home. Parmos, by the way, are a local delicacy in the north east, consisting of flattened meat, fried breadcrumbs, and melted cheese. Not the healthiest of foods, and completely alien to someone like Sarah as you can imagine. Very tasty though, all the same, more so after a good night out.

After some more drinks, the language would get a bit…well, saucier let's say. I would be dying with embarrassment, and chastising them, but Sarah would just laugh, while doing her best to cover Lorna's ears if she was in the vicinity. My dad would counteract these lowly shenanigans by quoting historical facts about Middlesbrough and its surrounding areas. He had got these from a book by Asa Briggs, the famous historian who had founded the Open

University. I hasten to add that this was one of the very few books my father had ever read. That and Dolly Parton's autobiography, as far as I'm aware. His main passion was still tinkering with his two bikes: a nineteen sixty three Lambretta from his Mod days, and a nineteen eighty Honda Gullwing, from when he converted to Country and Western- ism!

It was on the Saturday afternoon when my dad was impressing Sarah and Lorna with his bikes out in the backyard, that I spoke to my mother about my recent experiences and the appointment with Dr Marshall. I couldn't go into specific details with her, I just didn't think that she or my dad would understand.

'Your father won't give it too much thought,' she said. 'He loves his bikes and his music. Still loves the old comedies too. You know how he loves the daft stuff. Dafter the better. Yes,' she mused, 'He still misses those Chuckle Brothers. Daft old sod!'. That made me laugh and made it easier to talk. I felt that I *did* have to tell them about this condition though.

For someone who was normally so reticent

101

about these things, my mother was surprisingly open. I had already told them about having migraines and the usual, but unpleasant, run of the mill issues, but nothing about the visions, episodes, experiences. She spoke about her own experiences with migraines. Again, there was nothing strange or out of the ordinary with her. She even reiterated that to me. I told her in a vague, roundabout way about how I was 'receiving' my ideas for the stories.

She was only partly listening to me while I was quietly rambling on about 'brain fog', 'visual snow', and some other medical terms. I hadn't got to 'depersonalisation' and the other more worrying symptoms, and I honestly didn't know how I was going to try and explain these things to her when she started to talk about my grandfather. She sat down with her cup of tea and suddenly began to tell me about his experiences after the war.

Apparently, after coming home from Burma, he wasn't able to drive busses anymore, like he did before the war. That's why he was forced to change jobs and move down to

Redcar, where he started work cleaning out the blast furnaces in the steel works. Like me, and like my mother, he had also suffered with migraines, although I was soon to discover that his experiences were more similar to mine.

My grandfather had been a good boxer. He was the boxing champion of his battalion in fact, winning a big bout on the ship over to Burma. I knew that much. I still have his book about the legendary boxing trainer, Cus D'Amato, here in front of me. It has seen better days, I must say. I also knew that he was a keen chess player, and that he had won some county competitions when my mother was a small child. That didn't surprise me - he was an intelligent, self-educated man. I had been under the impression that he had taught himself how to play chess, or that he had been taught during his days in the army. However, my mother was about to enlighten me with some peculiar and very interesting facts.

She told me that he couldn't play chess before he joined the army. His best mate there was some sort of regional champion. A big

Welsh fellow he was, and they were close mates during the war. Those Celts tend to stick together. My grandfather found it fascinating when he would watch his friend play against the officers. He greatly admired how he would get the better of the upper classes without having to use his fists, or his brawn, or even money.

Anyway, my mother went on to tell me that one night, just before she was born, my grandfather went to bed early saying that he was ill.

'He was talking about seeing the Japanese flag and things in his vision. Weird stuff. Well, it must have been like those nasty zig zags things we get,' she said. 'Delayed shell-shock, your grandmother said it was. They didn't know anything about migraines back then really. And men especially didn't like to show any signs of weakness, not back then.'

She said that the night it started, he came downstairs 'in a bit of a stupor', as she put it; he walked past my grandmother and went into the kitchen. Then he got some of my mother's crayons and some card, sat at the table and began drawing chess moves out in front of him. My grandmother told her that it was the most peculiar thing. It was like he was sleep walking she said, but…he wasn't. I immediately thought of my trances, and those other migraine sufferers writing out formulae and compositions usually without knowing why.

This information about my grandfather was obviously a revelation to me. I was gobsmacked, and at the same time - I don't know…relieved? Continuing with this rare expression of openness, my mother then went into more detail.

'The thing is, he could only play those moves that he'd written out after one of his 'turns', as your grandmother called them. He did well while it lasted, but the other players soon found out that he was playing the same moves over and over. Used to get beaten all the time by the good players after that. He soon got fed up and went back into boxing for a while.'

'His experiences had given him a helping hand…strategies that improved his chess-playing abilities' I heard myself think out aloud.

My mother shook her head.

'Well no, he couldn't play chess before that!' she said.

This floored me, it really did.

'Temporary it was', she went on. 'Lasted a couple of years, that's all. From when it started, to when he packed it in.'

She finished her cuppa.

'You never told me any of this before,' I said to her.

'I never needed to,' she replied. 'Anyway, that's enough about the past. Me and your father are very proud of what you've achieved. That *Frozen Goods* play of yours looks like it's going to do well!'

Yes, even though there was a printout of an article about me and my forthcoming play from the paper framed on the mantlepiece in front of her, she was still referring to *Stolen Goods* as *Frozen Goods*. Bless her.

I spent the long journey back to Padstow just as preoccupied as I was on the journey from Leeds to my parents. I don't know what hit me the most…the openness of my mother during our conversation, the amazing facts about my grandfather's conditions, or the fact that it was only temporary. It lasted a couple of years or so, she had said. Was it going to be the same for me? It had been nearly that long since that first time in the hotel, but who was to say that would be the case for me?

I didn't know what to think anymore. Had his experiences darkened, then faded, like it appeared to be doing with me? I began to think of him going back into boxing. Now my mind really started to wonder - did he box to get hurt, to bring on pain…bring on his condition? My mother couldn't tell me that. Of course she couldn't. This was stupid! Fuck…I was getting carried away with all this again! Anyway, she had already told me far more than I had known before.

CHAPTER 7

By the time I met with Dr Marshall again, I had been taking the medication that she'd prescribed for nearly three weeks. Thankfully, the only side effects that I was experiencing was restlessness, and the odd bout of insomnia. It was during those nights that I would think and worry. Think about what I was going to do next, how would I come up with the material that would keep me going in the future. I was able to meet Dr Marshall in Exeter this time, which saved me travelling too far from home. I had been given the all-clear by my GP to drive again, so I went to see her.

Dr Marshall was pleased with how I was doing with the medication, and I explained that Sarah was also pleased. I was symptom free. A part of me was grateful, but deep down I felt something else. Looking back, I think it was resentfulness. It was a routine appointment, apart from when I mentioned what I had discovered about my grandfather. Dr Marshall was clearly interested in what I had to say, and asked my permission to do a comparative case study about our conditions in the future. I said that it was fine with me, but I would have to get clearance from my mother. I already knew that my mother would never agree to it. She liked to keep things under wraps and close to home, so I obviously wouldn't let her know about my latest conversation with the diminutive Dr Marshall.

A few more months passed before I actually got the chance to meet Jane Lilly in person. Her office had emailed me to say that she was in the UK for a short time before travelling to the States on business. Following the success of *Stolen Goods* as a radio broadcast, Jane had secured the rights for a television production version.

Filming would begin soon in Broxbourne in Scotland, of all places. Apparently, it was a quiet town east of Glasgow, now being used for film locations. George Clooney had discovered a large disused hospital there and used it in one of his movie's locations, so it was 'on the map'.

Jane had arranged for me and Sarah to attend the National TV awards in London the same weekend as our planned meeting. Travel, accommodation, expenses, everything would be taken cared of, her office assured me. I just had to get hold of a decent tuxedo, and Sarah an appropriate evening dress for the occasion.

Jane put us up in a lovely hotel, just down the road from her offices in Chiswick. We met her in the bar and restaurant on the ground floor. I had seen enough photos of Jane on the internet since our first conversation. She looked quite a bit like Joan Collins did at her age. She was pushing sixty, so I guessed that she'd had at least *some* work done to her, like most of them do to maintain a certain level of attractiveness. I'm sure Joan Collins did.

She greeted us with a well-spoken 'hello' and a polite handshake, before asking us about the our stay at the hotel. I'd been expecting 'darlings,' and a kisses-on-both-cheeks kind of greeting, something more befitting her telephone manner. She also gave me the usual

'Christ, you've done well!' look, after eyeing Sarah for a second or two,

Jane informed us that she was planning on doing a big launch for me at the hotel as soon as she got back from the States trip. She asked if we'd had the chance to do any shopping, sight-seeing etc, and how we were feeling about going to the TV awards the following day.

'Sarah and I are really looking forward it. It'll be a new experience for us,' I told her.

Sarah said how grateful we were for the invitation - a very kind gesture.

'Not at all', Jane replied. 'A bit of a taste of what's to come for you both, I'm sure!'

She seemed to have the ability to be sincere, and yet slightly condescending at the same time. She also appeared to be less…how can I put it…complimentary, gushing even … since our initial conversation. Maybe it was because she now 'owned' me…in a manner of speaking. I couldn't help but think how great it must be in her position.

That subtle yet menacing trait of female envy towards another attractive woman was palpable from Jane during the meeting. I have to admit that Jane was almost as eye catching as Sarah, but older of course. She looked every inch the jet setting agent, with an air of someone who had been around money and success throughout her life. If I'm being honest, I felt both in awe of her and intimidated by her.

After the initial chat over a drink about how well *Stolen Goods* seemed to be doing, and the forthcoming press campaign, Jane told me that *Going Somewhere* was now also up for a weekly series on BBC 4 Extra. One of Jane's contacts had mentioned the possibilities of touting *Going Somewhere?* as a short independent piece at the next Sundance Film Festival. Sarah and I just looked at each other in amazement at this.

'God, that's fantastic news!' I said.

'Well, let's just see the outcome of that first,' Jane replied calmly.

'So, back to this radio series,' she went on. 'It's going to have an all-female cast, instead of the all-male cast in your original story. Keeping in line with the times. We've got two up and coming Irish actresses. They're very keen about the project…working on something with gravitas. You're ok with that I'm sure?'

I was just about to make one of my ill-judged and outdated jokes, when Sarah suddenly coughed and gripped my hand under the table. I had lost count how many times she had been forced to do that with me.

Then Jane turned to the serious business of my deal with her. She reminded me that she was expecting the further four concepts, scripts etc as agreed in my contract. She did add that there would be some leniency there, but she followed that with saying that I was to provide her with at least one strong, workable concept in the immediate future. Something sellable, and along the same lines as *Stolen Goods* and *Going Somewhere?* She gave me a stern look as she told me this.

Call me over-sensitive, but at that moment, I seemed to detect the tyrannical undertones that had made her father such a feared and formidable business man. That's what you need in an agent, I suppose. All the same, my sphincter muscle began to twitch quite a bit, and I could feel myself breaking into a bit of a sweat. Everything around me seemed to be speeding up. *'Get a grip on yourself for fuck's sake,'* I could hear myself thinking.

I looked at Sarah, who was now calmly and happily speaking to Jane about the TV award ceremony at the O2 Arena the next day. Household names and well known television programmes were being discussed by them. Jane was giving away the odd lesser-known and racy facts about certain celebrities, Sarah was telling her about how sitting down with a glass of wine and watching celebrity shows like *Strictly Come Dancing* and *Dancing on Ice* were her guilty pleasures, when I suddenly heard myself blurting out the words, *'Dancing on Spice!'*

I couldn't believe what I had just said. They both looked at me in astonishment. Sarah just stared down at the floor, while Jane coolly asked me what I was talking about.

'Just an idea,' I muttered back to her. 'You know...kids, perhaps famous kids, no, they'll have to be really hard up…a bit of social realism, something topical…'

Sarah coughed nervously again, but it was too late this time. Jane gave me a look as if to say, *'Fucking ell…are you the same guy who wrote these stories?'* But I went on, 'Yes…they're cast aside by society, then forced onto dangerous drugs and pushed into doing a crazy TV show…like that film *The Running Man*…that was a book to begin with you know…Well, these kids take the drug spice, then…then they see how long they can dance…on ice before they collapse in a stupor…'

That piece of poorly-timed gibberish was followed by a moment or two of painful silence. Then Jane swiftly finished her drink, made her excuses, and made her exit from the building.

CHAPTER 8

When we got back from the TV awards, I decided to stop taking my meds. That evening, and the meeting with Jane, did it for me. I had to prove to her that I wasn't a fluke, a joke... I was going to show her, provide her with something special again. Just one more idea...maybe two...no, there you go, you see...

I hadn't had a 'helping hand', not even as much as a bit of a headache, since my first meeting with Dr Marshall, but I was already pushing things again. Going behind Sarah's back, opening myself and my family up to all sorts of problems.

And the TV awards...I wasn't the same after that. Jane was right, I had a taste of what was to come, what I...sorry, I mean *we* could have. And what a taste it was. The O2 Arena decked out and lit up for this glitzy annual occasion. The stars, the food, the drinks, being treated like stars ourselves. There were so many familiar faces, I wouldn't know where to start. Then seeing Lorna's face when we brought back the selfies and the signed photos of Ant and Dec for her....not every father gets the chance to experience that in his lifetime.

Back in our everyday lives, Sarah was making excuses for me as usual, for the meeting, and my increasingly capricious behaviour. She blamed the tablets; she obviously didn't know was that I had stopped taking them. I didn't feel guilty though ...why? I started to ask myself if there was a purpose behind all of this... getting carried away.

Even though Sarah had continued to support me, put up with my nonsense whilst still trying to live her own busy life, it was becoming apparent that I was wearing her down. Slowly but surely. That inner calmness, that innate positivity, and ability to put up with things, see things through, was beginning to wear away. Yes, she was enjoying meeting all these people, and seeing my achievements, but it wasn't that important to her.

What was becoming more important to me than Sarah having her husband back, was showing Jane what I...well not exactly me, but what could be delivered to her. Although at the end of the day, I didn't even need to. The worse that could happen really would be the contract ending. I'd still get some of the rights. We could have lived comfortably as a family, had another child even. No, I had to go further. There again, once you've rubbed shoulders with Judie Dench, Ant and Dec, that girl from Countdown.... well, for me anyway, things would never be the same.

As I was surreptitiously devising some kind of plan to get my episodes back, I couldn't help but think about what my mother had told me about my grandfather again. It was temporary for him, and I was pretty certain that he wasn't getting any medical help. Well, nothing like the kind of assistance that I'd been receiving. So what about the boxing? He had retired from that years before. Why suddenly get back into it? Was he planning to get hurt...to get hurt quickly?

That must have been it! I thought to myself, as I eyed up Lorna's old toy hammer in my now seriously-underused writing shed. I didn't have much time left, if I was going by my grandfather's timeline. I had to act, and I had to act pronto. Contact sports…that was a good start. Yes, I would join a club…boxing, martial arts. Bring it on!

I wasn't in the best of shapes at that point. In fact, I had lost that swimmer's physique a while ago. I was a beanpole with a paunch. I thought that might go in my favour, you know, throwing myself into sparring with fit and strong men…and women. My grandfather took me to the local boxing gym when I was about twelve years old. Some kid punched me in the stomach and winded me. I burst into tears, and my mother went berserk when we got home. Stopped me going again. I wish she hadn't.

Anyway, here I was in my late thirties, throwing myself into as many different classes as I could, with the mad intention of getting hit in the head. Within the space of a couple of months, I was banned from every martial arts class in a ten mile radius of my house. Posters were placed around the foyers of the gyms and community centres, warning classes of a mad man picking fights; their social media sites also had a description of me, followed by the same warning. The police even contacted me with an unofficial caution one afternoon when Sarah was running the craft stall, and Lorna was in school. How I'd kept it from them so far had been a small miracle.

All the same, it had already become very difficult for Sarah. I was so obsessed with coming up with ideas and all that shit, and so preoccupied with myself, my creativity, or lack of it, and my career, or what was going to be left of it, that she was clearly feeling neglected. Of course, I didn't notice this at the time, being so immersed in my own problems. The only way I had been able to attend these futile classes was by telling her that I was playing squash and going to meetings. God forbid if she knew that I was going through all this madness, let alone stopping my medication. Then one day, it finally all came to a head.

I remember that afternoon well, unfortunately. It was sunny, an autumnal sun, but quite cold and windy. Sarah was out doing one of those cold water swims with her posh friends down the bay. I had just spent an inane half hour or so in that pathetically titled 'writing shed', either playing darts, or doodling pictures of cars and buildings, or even male and female genitalia, just like a bored schoolboy would. I knew that Sarah would be home shortly, before getting changed and taking Lorna to her football training.

I had decided to nip back into the kitchen to get myself a sly little alcoholic beverage, when I saw Sarah standing there with the two cockerpoos, Mable and Matilda, at her feet. She was still wearing the dry robe, the big woolly bobble hat, a pair of walking boots and thick woollen socks. She just stood there staring at me with a face like thunder. I was trying to work out why, when I noticed in the corner of the room a split-open bin liner, the one I had forgotten to take out that morning. Spilling out of it onto the floor were some used kitchen towels, tea bags, wet wipes, and at least two weeks-worth of my medication, still in its packaging.

I just froze. Talk about brain fog. I honestly did not know what to say or do next. Those fucking dogs! I bet it was Matilda, that fucking dog never liked me from day one! I found it difficult to swallow, before I tried to make some kind of pitiful excuse for my incredibly stupid and irresponsible behaviour.

However, Sarah didn't give me the chance. She just snapped…big time. I suppose all those years of listening to my stupidity, putting up with my pretentious nonsense and bullshit, all of it came out then and there. She flew into a rage that I have to say I had never witnessed in all the years I had known her, never mind been married to her. I really shit myself at this point, couldn't get a word in edgeways. What was the point anyway…what was I going to say to her?

She spent the next ten minutes calling me all the lying, inconsiderate and stupid bastards under the sun, along with throwing a few dishes my way. She was completely right of course. I did manage to speak…only this made the situation even worse.

Did I apologise? No. Did I do my best to explain what I was doing, and why, as clearly and as calmly as I could at that moment? No. Like the complete and utter selfish twat that I had become by then, I went all nasty, I went on the attack. I heard myself calling *her* selfish and inconsiderate. I went on about my achievements with the stories and the publishing deal, how I had provided for both her and Lorna, how I was going to continue to provide them with more and more, with greater and better things, with a better lifestyle.

Sarah screamed back that she didn't give a shit about all those things...Jane Lilly, the luvvies and darlings, the soap stars, the TV awards, all this talk of success, she just wanted things to be back as they were. Jesus Christ, she was crying as well at this point. Instead of stopping it there, what did I do?...what did I fucking do?

I launched back at her about being able to swan around with her fucking divvy, snobby-nosed friends, doing silly stuck up, posh things like hanging around the beach sipping flat whites, whilst wearing those stupid fucking gowns...or robes...or whatever the fuck they were, and those daft woollen hats!

It was after that cruel barrage of unfair insults that I saw a look in Sarah's eyes, her beautiful eyes, that genuinely frightened me. Then came that kick. That kick from those heavily-booted size seven feet, straight into my testicles. That was something I will never...no, I will be unable to forget.

It was a pain that I had never felt before. All those sayings and stories that are commonly used about losing the family jewels, about having your balls kicked through the roof of your mouth...well, they suddenly made sense. I felt at once emasculated, and wondering if they were ever there to begin with. Sarah stormed out of the house as I slowly crawled into the living room. I felt sick and faint as I lay on the living room floor. I couldn't make it onto the sofa. I took deep breaths and tried my best to compose myself...then it happened.

Lying flat out on the living room floor, grimacing through that terrible pain, eyes partly shut, I suddenly noticed those familiar patterns emerging in my left eye. Was it actually starting to happen, or was it just shock? No, it was happening. It felt like it had been so long since my last episode, but I still *almost* knew what to expect. I winced in discomfort as the visual snow, and the other more common symptoms that I could now give a name to, led me to the strange and bizarre journey that I hoped was ahead.

The faces greeted me at the gate, the void grew bigger, filling space in my head, my mind's eye. Nothing haunting this time. I was there, before I knew it, in a fantastical adventure. Just like the bizarre experiences that had spawned *Stolen Goods*, and *Going Somewhere?* on those first couple of occasions, I was again receiving something from deep within my own psyche.

The shapes and figures started to act the scenes out before me. Jagged, yet somehow clear formations. They were just like they had appeared to me before. The Zoetrope effect, the lines, the cylinder…everything. But then I felt the hypnotic pressure of the sudden need to sleep overcoming me. The story hadn't reached its conclusion yet, but I was struggling to stay conscious. The scene, the characters, the faces, the void...everything was slipping away from me. I think I even remember trying to grip my testicles in order to keep me awake, to sustain the experience, but it was no use. I awoke in the same position on the living room floor. Opening my eyes, I found myself staring up at the ceiling again.

After a moment or two, I managed to drag myself up off the floor and onto the sofa. Jesus, my balls were really aching. In fact, my whole groin felt like it had been used as a punchbag. Sitting there on the sofa with my trousers and underpants around my ankles in order give myself some much needed space, I realised that I only had half, if not just part, of a story. Still, I had to hurry and get down what I had been given before I had forgotten that much of it. At least this time I hadn't pissed myself.

I eventually made my way back into the kitchen, where I filled a bowl with water and ice. As I gently lowered my now deformed looking testicles into the bowl of iced water, I dictated this latest and unexpected adventure onto my phone. Feeling that soothing effect of the ice cold water helped to calm me down. I even had a bit of a giggle to myself about my mother saying *Frozen Goods* instead of *Stolen Goods*. She wasn't far wrong...yes, you could add *Swollen Goods* to that, I laughed to myself, before wincing again in pain.

It didn't take long to finish my dictation: it was only half a story. All the same, I wasn't thinking about Sarah and Lorna. I wasn't thinking about the fact that Sarah had found out that I had been incredibly stupid, selfish, and irresponsible. I wasn't even thinking about the fact that my marriage was now clearly in serious trouble. No, all I could think about was how and from where I was going to get the rest of this story.

Then it came to me...another fucking stupid and ridiculous idea! Yes of course, it was that swift and powerful kick in the nuts that just did it. It wasn't a blow to the head. All those

127

hours I had spent picking fights with black belts and boxers…even hitting myself on the side of the head with Lorna's old toy hammer, it had all been a waste of time. In my increasingly deluded and desperate state, I figured that the answer to my problems was *another* great kick in my testicular region! *How was I going to achieve this?* I asked myself. I couldn't go back to the gyms and clubs again, and I certainly couldn't ask Sarah. Although that did actually enter my hopeless mind for a second. I couldn't just pick fights on the street, I would get arrested, or beaten up, or both. No, I would have to get the ball rolling…. excuse the pun…find some other way to get this deed done, and soon!

CHAPTER 9

I was back living with my parents after that. Thankfully, I was able to say goodbye to Lorna, who was upset, but very understanding, especially for a child of her age. Although Sarah wouldn't speak to me. She just left a note saying that she wanted me out for the foreseeable future. She also laid down some ground rules that I would have to comply with before she would even consider me coming back home. Namely, getting back on the medication, seeking professional help, coming to some kind of arrangement with Jane Lilly about the termination of my contract, and last but not least, going back to some kind of steady, conventional work like teaching.

Well as you can imagine by now, as much as I loved my wife and daughter, these considerations were taking a back seat. What was paramount to me at that point was finishing this story. In other words, getting my nuts smashed in again.

My parents were *not* impressed with me! They knew this screwed-up situation had been caused by my stupidity and selfishness. Like I said, they genuinely thought a lot of Sarah, and they obviously adored Lorna, their own grandchild. Not a day went by without them mentioning this to me, along with the odd speech about gift horses and all that. They had always gone on about gift horses to me since I had met Sarah.

My mother knew that something else was up though. Call it women's intuition, or maybe it was because I had opened up to her about the whole migraine condition. I should also point out that I was still hobbling around at this point, tenderly holding my groin whilst wincing with pain every few minutes. For whatever reason, my dear old mother knew that something was up. She didn't say anything to me, but then again, she didn't need to either. Most of the time the atmosphere there was as cold as that bowl of water I...well, you get the picture.

I had only been up there a few days when Richard called me. I was quite surprised to hear from him. I told him that I was visiting my parents. I made up some bullshit story about my father needing help with some documents and paperwork. I was getting good at bullshitting now. Richard said that it was a nice coincidence, serendipitous even, that I was up in Redcar. He was eager to meet me after things had taken off with Jane and the plays and the rest of it. After all, he had helped me get there to begin with. As messed up as I had become, I still questioned whether that had been a good thing or not. I was happy to meet up with him though. It would get me out, and hopefully take my mind off things, maybe provide me with some solace, even some inspiration.

We met at the same place as before. I wasn't driving, which was the only sensible thing I was doing at this point. The bus taking me into town was slightly late. When I walked - I mean limped - into the brasserie, Richard was already seated with a drink for each of us. He was immaculately turned out and as chipper as ever. I looked like the dishevelled and preoccupied mess that I had become.

131

'Christ, what happened to you?' he asked, as I slowly lowered myself into my seat.

'Don't tell me you've visited one of those dominatrices around here?'

I asked him what he meant, before making up a lie about having a nasty fall in my parent's kitchen.

'A bit of ball busting it looks like, from the way you struggled in here and sat down!' he said with a chuckle.

'And now you look like you've just seen a ghost!' he added, when he saw the look on my face.

I asked him, nervously, what he meant by 'ball busting'. That's when he went on to explain this weird, sadomasochist perversion that some men are inclined to, having pain inflicted on them.

That was it...that was the answer! I thought to myself. *I'll pay a visit to one of these mean ladies, get my bollocks kicked in. That would surely do the job...bring on another migraine episode so that I could finish the rest of my latest gift!*

Richard might as well had been talking to himself from that point on and during the rest of our lunch. I was miles away, thinking about this ball busting thing. I continued to nod politely and grimace in pain as he told me about trying to get his new play off the ground. I did hear him ask me about Jane and the TV awards, and the production work that was being negotiated. His envy of my 'achievements' was palpable now, saying things like 'man of the moment', and 'Jane's favourite' with a quite substantial dig in my side.

'Anything else in that productive pipeline of yours?' he asked as we were leaving.

Pipeline...fucking 'ell, if he only knew!

As soon as I got back to my folks' place, I started doing some research on this ball busting thing. Like most men on the planet, I was no stranger to pornography, but I have to admit this was all new to me. BDSM, sub genres, testicular torture methods...it was all there. Men in cowboy hats, gimp masks, top hats, Nazi outfits (Hitler was a notorious *ball bustee*), sometimes naked, sometimes semi naked, being

133

kicked, beaten and stomped on by women (in some cases men), dressed in equally bizarre clothing.

Whips, latex, and stiletto-heeled thigh high boots seemed to be the most common form of dress for the Mistresses, along with the odd schoolgirl outfit. The Japanese were also on there, taking this torturous act to another level of pain and sadomasochism as you would expect from them. *Tamakeri* it's called out there apparently. They even had men tied up with ropes gripped around their private parts in order to get more pain from this already brutal act.

I also read an article that mentioned the significant health risks posed to the male during these acts. That was understandable, but I just wanted a good old fashioned kick in the balls ... with a size seven walking boot if possible. It would be clean, quick and secretive. I could tell her what I wanted, and how I wanted it done. Brilliant. Yep, I was so far gone now, that I was actually getting excited about paying a strange woman to kick me in my testicles as hard as she could whilst wearing a pair of chunky, size seven walking boots, just like Sarah had been wearing on that day.

The next step was finding someone appropriate for the job. I typed Dominatrix North East England into the search engine; there were loads on there: big ones, small ones, cute ones, scary ones. I chose one by her destination. This one was based in Scarborough. Close enough, but also far enough not to complicate the issue. It was a two and a half hour train journey from Redcar via York. I had a read through the profile of this particular dominatrix: Mistress Kimberly, experienced forty three year old, auburn hair, shapely, five feet seven inches tall. That was very close to Sarah's build. Ball busting was there on her list of specialities, along with flogging, humiliation, foot fetish, Sissy training, pegging…need I go on? Her fee was the standard two hundred pounds for an hourly session.

I paid on my card straight away for the three-till-four slot the following Monday, which was four days away. I also added the walking boots to the 'special requirements' box. Then I booked my train tickets and waited anxiously for the day to come.

On the train, I had plenty of time to think about what was going on in my life at that point. Yes, it really was a mess. It was a fair journey to Scarborough. Being really nervous seemed to prolong it. I was very tempted to get off at York and get the next train home. But I did manage to hold my nerve, because I had convinced myself that this was the right thing to do.

What was keeping me going then, though, was the certainty in my mind that this latest plan of mine was going to solve everything. My marriage would be put back on track once I was able to get another idea to Jane. Everyone would have faith in me again. I emailed Jane's office to find out how the progress of *Stolen Goods* as well as *Going Somewhere?* was going. That meeting with her at the hotel, before I got nervous and made that ridiculous pitch to her, had got me really revved up. Especially when she mentioned the Sundance Film Festival thing. I also told her in the email that I had something special 'in the pipeline' as Richard had put it. After that, I had a drink from the buffet, and tried my best to chill out for a while.

Mistress Kimberly's place was about a mile from Scarborough station. So, armed with a tube of anti-inflammatory gel and some loosely-fitting incontinence pants, just in case of any unwanted accidents, I made my way to the taxi rank across the road from the station. I had to get a taxi, because I was still walking with a limp. One of them still hadn't come down yet from that kick Sarah had so graciously given me.

   The taxi driver raised his eyebrows when I gave him the address. I gave him the money and told him to get on with the driving. The house was quite close to the seafront. It was in the middle of a neat row of terraced houses that were set apart from the quiet road by a small courtyard. I noticed a basement floor below as I paid the driver and made my way to the property. I rang the doorbell and Mistress

Kimberly answered within a few seconds. She was very polite and well spoken. Nothing like I had expected. I immediately thought that she looked too classy and attractive to be doing what she was doing, but there again, there was a wide range of women involved in this kind of work. And it *was* work at the end of the day.

I was led upstairs, not down to the basement as you would expect one of these dungeons, or sex dens, to be. We went into what seemed like a spare room. *'I bet that's got a nice sea view,'* I found myself thinking as I looked at the deep red, heavily curtained window. It was quite dimly lit. The walls were also red, but a lighter shade of red than the curtains. A few erotic artwork prints, like pictures from a really old *Karma Sutra,* were hung on the walls. Rows of tall candles were dotted around the place, some musky with incense; along with an exotic-looking lamp, these provided the room with a sultry air. There was a vintage-style single bed in the corner, which I found a bit strange, but there you go.

Some paraphernalia was hooked on the bed poles: chains, handcuffs, whips, gloves, gimp masks, run of the mill stuff I suppose. Two shelves were full of sex toys of various shapes and sizes, for both male and female by the looks of them. A web cam was strategically placed at the bottom of the bed. Big business these days. Still, a bit sparse for a dominatrix's den maybe? There again, what would I know?

'So, let me get this right,' Mistress Kimberly said as she checked her watch.

'You just want me to put on these walking boots and kick you in the balls as hard as I can? No tying you up, or constricting your genitalia, no stomping, spitting or pegging?'

I confirmed that was all I had in mind. She wouldn't have to change into any special gear or anything, just a good old fashioned ball buster for me.

'Well,' I added, 'you could call me a stupid, selfish and pretentious twat whilst you do it. That might help a bit.'

She smiled and nodded at this request.

'Oh, just one more thing,' I said as she sat

139

on the bed, putting on the walking boots that I had paid for her to get.

'I have to keep my trousers on. It's important...for research you see. They're quite loose fitting as you can see.'

She didn't look so happy about that and said that it would probably make the whole ball busting business trickier, and possibly less effective. She got off the bed, shrugged her shoulders and said that I was paying for a service, and I would get it.

Once she was on her feet, she told me to stand in the middle of the room with my legs apart and my hands behind my head. She did insist that I wore a gag, because I was likely to scream out in pain. Fair enough, I suppose. I couldn't help but sense that she was as nervous as I was at this point. All the same, as long as she did her job I didn't really care. Then before I knew it, Mistress Kimberly had taken a step back, before racing forward and putting her boot-clad foot into my groin area. Only, she didn't quite hit the spot. No, believe or not, she managed to clobber my Old Boy and the top of my right thigh. Fucking 'ell, I couldn't believe it! Now I had a mangled knob along with a pair of deformed looking testicles!

'What the fuck are you doing?' I shouted, after I had spat out the gag and dropped to the floor.

'I'm so sorry, but I've never done this bit before,' she replied.

I asked her what the hell she meant by that, being that it was her job and she had advertised this service. She went on to tell me that she had only been doing the real kinky stuff for a few weeks. Apparently she had taken over as a favour from her friend who had gone into porn films big time over in eastern Europe.

'I just used to do cam work, escorting, girlfriend experience stuff before that,' she said timidly.

'Aw, fucking great!' I yelled, as I picked myself up off the floor, clutching my now beyond-repair nether regions.

'You're telling me that I've come all this way for a second-rate service!'

I was becoming aggressive now. Mistress Kimberly was aware of it too. She offered to give it another go. I shouted at her that she had no option. I had gone there to get my balls busted, and I was bloody well going to have them busted ... inexperienced or not! I got to my feet as quickly as I could. Jesus, I was struggling with the pain. My right thigh was numb, and probably covered in bruises.

'You're going to pass out!' she said.

'Just get on with it...you...you useless slut!' I yelled pack at her. I was spitting out my words in a maddened rage.

Before I knew it, she had taken another small run-up and kicked out at me. Then she raced out of the room crying, leaving me writhing in agony on the floor again. I had never made a woman cry in my life before. Now I had two of them balling... sorry - crying their eyes out in front of me within a few weeks of each other! One of them my wife, and one a crap dominatrix. What had I become?

This time, she had connected with them...my testicles that is. As painful as the first kick was, I hadn't felt *this* kind of sickening discomfort since I'd had the full might of Sarah's deft touch. I really was a freak of nature now...and not for the reasons that I had thought before!

Everything began to throb and cramp up as I lay there waiting for something...anything. Yes, anything would do now. Just a vision...a face...a glimpse of an ending, especially after this debacle. I waited ... and waited ... for what seemed like an eternity. Of course, it was probably only ten minutes or so.

And nothing happened. *Nothing fucking happened.* Not even the slightest sign of a migraine. I was done. After another few minutes, I realised that I was still alone in the room. Mistress Kimberly had buggered off somewhere. This was turning into a nightmare, only I was soon to find out that the nightmare had just begun.

CHAPTER 10

I dragged myself up off the floor. I had never
been in so much pain in my life. Just as I
attempted to leave, two large policemen barged
their way into the room. Mistress Kimberly was
just behind them yelling,

'There he is, the bastard!'

They grabbed hold of me and pushed me
through the door. One of the policemen
punched me in the face. He gave me this look
as if to make out that it was personal. I had the
feeling that he was a familiar face in that house.
They hauled me down the stairs and into the
back of a police van. I couldn't believe that this
was happening to me. I only wanted to get an
end to a story, that's all.

I was suddenly aware of a number of
people stopping in the street and coming out
onto their doorsteps in order to witness this
freak show that I had now become.

'I didn't ask for this ... you don't
understand, I didn't ask for this!' I hollered as

they bundled me into the back of the van headfirst.

'Well, you seemed to pay enough for it!' the officer who had given me the right hook sniggered. The other officer was busy on his phone, doing a search on my identity by the looks of it.

After spending another four humiliating hours at the police station, I was released with a caution. They told me I was lucky not to get arrested. I think they actually felt sorry for me when they found out who I was, and saw the state I was in. I was in *real* pain now and struggling to walk even more than before. They had to get a medic to me while I was at the station. There was blood in my urine, my right thigh was black and blue, and my genitalia looked like they had belonged to the Elephant Man. Oh, and I had a black eye on the right hand side just to top it off. It was from that hook from the cop. Incidentally, I think that may have helped in me getting a caution, rather than being arrested.

The train journey back to Middlesbrough seemed to take forever. Everything was going through my head, just about everything that had happened to me since these fucking migraines had started. And on top of that I was in so much physical pain. I'm not ashamed to say that I wept for the last half hour of the journey. The only thing keeping me going at that point was making it all up to Sarah, promising her that it was all behind me. I would have to prove that all this madness was over now, thank God. I would contact Jane and tell her that I was not going to be able to provide her with any further work, whatever the consequences. It *was* a fluke, and frankly I didn't care anymore. I just wanted my life and my family back.

I didn't mention anything to my parents the following morning. They had both been asleep by the time I had eventually got in the previous night. They were shocked when they saw me. I did what I did best now, by making up another bullshit story about fighting off two muggers at the end of my night out with some old friends in town. I said two muggers just to make it sound more impressive in front of my father. I don't suppose that he gave a shit by now though.

I was just about to sit down for my breakfast when my phone rang. I didn't recognise the number, so I decided to answer it, just in case it was a business call, or maybe Sarah, Tim, or Lorna had changed their numbers. Unfortunately, it wasn't any of them.

No, it was a reporter from one of the big redtop daily papers. They wanted to know if I would comment on the story they were about to publish about my wild and kinky nights with a dominatrix from Scarborough.

I nearly spat my coffee out, then I almost choked on it. I felt sick as I asked him who he was, and what he was talking about. He just went on about the story, embellishing so many things there and then on the phone. I thought that I was going to pass out. I made some pathetic and futile attempt to correct him, even lie a bit, threaten legal action, but he was too quick and experienced for me. He just told me

147

to expect some unwanted coverage once the story was published the next morning.

I was just trying to get my head around the appalling consequences that all this was going to have on my life and my family, when my phone rang again. It was Jane Lilly this time. I almost filled my trousers when I saw her number, and I had thought that the days of the incontinence pants were behind me! I can make a joke of it now, because I have nothing to lose. Back then though, well that was the worse day of my life…so far.

Jane went fucking BALLISTIC! (Sorry, that really was an unintended reference to balls again). Those tyrannical undertones that I had sensed in the past came right to the surface now. She called me all the stupid, pitiful bastards going. Who was I to argue? I just had to sit there and let her go on with her tirade.

'Do you have any idea what this has done for the agency's reputation?' she howled at me.

'Threatening prostitutes in this day and age? You can't even tap a barmaid on the arse without getting the book thrown at you!'

I managed to get a word in edgeways and explained that she wasn't a prostitute, she was an inexperienced dominatrix, and that I was only there to conduct research for a new script that I was working on. There was silence on the other side of the line, followed by a long intake of breath and a biblical sized sigh. Believe it or not, I was actually just about to tell her that I had this brilliant new play called *Stollen Goods*. It was a sequel to *Stolen Goods* set in a winter wonderland, what with Christmas only a few months away. Before I got the chance, Jane went to town on me again.

'You damned fool…are you not aware of the #metoo movement…my God man, it's lucky for you that they didn't lock you up! You're not a politician, no amount of spin could turn this around. That poor wife and daughter of yours! I should have known that you were an idiot back in the hotel when you came up with that ridiculous 'Dancing on Spice'…*idea*…for want of a better word. Well, you're finished in this business as far as I'm concerned. Do not try to contact me, or my office. My legal team will be in touch!'

She actually said more than that, but I've done my best to blank out much of the torrent of abuse that she laid at my door. Anyway, that was the last I heard from Jane Lilly. I heard quite a bit from her solicitors, though, over the following months.

Next to call was my father in law, Tim. Now as I have already mentioned, Tim was a very fair minded and understanding man, just as his daughter was a fair minded and understanding woman. However, just like Sarah, he wasn't one to be messed around with. He began the conversation very calmly, but when I said that I was going to speak to Sarah, he blew his top. He accused me of being all the stupid (yes, that word was thrown about a bit), sick, perverted, and selfish bastards under the sun. He did accept that I had this very peculiar condition that had obviously thrown our lives into turmoil, but he was first and foremost the protective father.

How could I blame him? It must have come out about the first ball busting incident with Sarah as well, because he said something about not realising that I was the aggressive type. He ended the call by telling me that neither Sarah nor Lorna wanted to see or speak to me, and that they had now changed their phone numbers and come off social media. Oh, he also informed me that as much as he pitied me, if I did try and contact, or come near his daughter and granddaughter without their permission, he would do more than bust my balls…he would kill me with his bare hands.

After that call I wept for days. The story came out the following day, just as the reporter said it would. It was only on page five of that particular daily paper to begin with, but once the story broke, it went viral over the next week or so. It even made the television regional news channels in both the Teesside and the Southwest areas, my homes respectively.

CHAPTER 11

It's pissing down again today. It's rained for days actually, which is a rare sight over here. Grey, windy, and miserable. By 'here', I mean Andalusia, Costa Del Sol, Malaga to be more precise. I moved over here with my parents a couple of months after the story broke.

It became unbearable. My poor mother and father became sucked into the nightmare, along with Sarah, Lorna and Tim. My parents had been eyeing up an apartment in Benalmadena for some time, but this pushed them into moving over there for good. Two staunch Brexit voters moving to the continent...you couldn't write it, they said.

Thankfully they hadn't lost their sense of humour, or their strong wills. They stuck by me through it all, but there again, I suppose they had to. I had no one else. There's talk of some kind of a lockdown in Spain. A virus from China looks like it's really getting out of hand now in parts of Europe. God help the UK with that goon squad government in charge.

The press really went to town on me. They started off by saying that I had been visiting prostitutes for years, not just to get my kicks, in the literal sense, but to get inspiration for my writing. That made me think that it must have been the nasty cop who gave away my details and all the rest of it to the press. And that's when they gave me the title 'Kinky Playwright'.

Within a matter of days, there was crap all over the internet about me being involved in cults, and all kinds of nasty shit. I've only spoken to Sarah once since the story broke, and that was to discuss the finalising of the divorce. She's with Tim's mate now, the Kung Fu Barrister. Jesus, what a cruel twist that was.

Lorna - well, I haven't seen or spoken to her. She told her mother that I make her sick to her stomach. She's also been forced to change school twice because of harassment from other kids about me. Must be incredibly difficult for her, especially since she's not long become a teenager.

I know now that I should have thought about my beautiful wife and child, about what I already had. But no, I thought that I had been given something special, and I promised them something special. I paid for that with my life. Not in the fatal sense. No. I gave everything away at that point. I should have put these experiences behind me, admitted that they were over, that it had been some bizarre 'gift'. Should have listened to everyone else: Sarah, Tim, Dr Marshall, even my mother when she told me that my grandfather's condition was temporary. Stupid, greedy fool.

It's all too late now. Hindsight is a wonderful thing as they say, but it can be as cruel as any kind of man-made torture in circumstances like mine. After all, I didn't possess a great mind, just a strange one. What would anyone else do? A gift that turned into a life shattering curse!

Dostoevsky was wrong when he said that fools and scoundrels are the only ones who make it beyond forty. Just one last quote from me, then I'm done. Really…done. It's from that old Cus D'Amato book that my grandfather left me. I was looking through it earlier, thinking about him and everyone else that I have ever loved. *'Nothing is ever as bad as the imagination makes it, not even death.'* Well, there will be no more imagining from me. No…more….imagining…..

Acknowledgements

Once again, I would like to thank my parents, whose support and encouragement have enabled me to achieve this, my second publication.

Thank you to all those who read my drafts and have given me their honest feedback, in particular to Jamie Lewellyn, who really helped with earlier drafts, by telling me whether it was *'good ... or shit!'*

At this point, I would like to acknowledge and thank my former lecturers, who greatly inspired me: Fiona Reid, Norry LaPorte, Mark Diamond, Gareth Williams and Des Barry.

T.G. Hyde
June 2022